Five Doubts

———

Mary Caponegro

MARSILIO
PUBLISHERS
NEW YORK

Five Doubts

Printed in the United States of America

ISBN 1-56886-059-5

Marsilio Publishers
853 Broadway
New York, New York 10003
marsiliopublishers.com

Marsilio Publishers' titles are distributed by
Consortium Book Sales & Distribution (800-283-3572)

Segments of this book appeared in literary magazines in somewhat different form: The Spectacle in
The Iowa Review, An Etruscan Catechism in *Italian Americana,* Il Libro dell'Arte, Tombola, and Doubt
Uncertainty Possibility Desire (excerpted) in *Conjunctions.* The author is grateful to those editors,
David Hamilton, Lee Montgomery, Carol Bonomo Albright, and especially Bradford Morrow (who
championed this fiction through thick and thin), as well as to the American Academy in Rome, The
Academy/Institute of Arts and Letters, and Hobart & William Smith Colleges, for their generous sup-
port during the many stages of this project's evolution.

Library of Congress Cataloging-in-Publication Data

Caponegro, Mary, 1956-
Five Doubts / Mary Caponegro
p. cm.
ISBN 1-56886-059-5 (pbk.: alk. paper)
1. Experimental fiction, American. 2. Artists--Fiction. 3. Art--Fiction. I. Title.
PS3553.A5877F58 1998
813'.54--dc21
98-37692
CIP

for John Hawkes (1925-1998)
who taught me the language of story
and never ceased turning doubt into art

CONTENTS

TABLE OF IMAGES

A) Manuscript page of Cennino d'Andrea Cennini's Il Libro dell'Arte

B) Mosaic from the "Great Hunting Room" of Piazza Armerina, Sicily

C) Neapolitan Tombolone Board

D) Tarquinian tomb painting: Tomba degli Auguri

E) Detail from Andrea del Verrochio's Baptism of Christ

Finito Il Di: 4 —

Mes: P:o, 1737. —

When you wish to see whether the general effect of your picture corresponds with that of the object represented after nature take a mirror and set it so that it reflects the actual thing, and then compare the reflection with your picture, and consider carefully whether the subject of the two images is in conformity with both, studying especially the mirror. The mirror ought to be taken as a guide—that is, the flat mirror— for within its surface substances have many points of resemblance to a picture; namely, that you see the picture made upon one plane showing things which appear in relief, and the mirror upon one plane does the same. The picture is one single surface, and the mirror is the same.

The picture is intangible, inasmuch as what appears round and detached cannot be enclosed within the hand, and the mirror is the same. The mirror and the picture present the images of things surrounded by shadow and light, and each alike seems to project considerably from the plane of its surface. And since you know that the mirror presents detached things to you by means of outlines and shadows and lights, and since you have moreover amongst your colors more powerful shadows and lights than those of the mirror, it is certain that if you but know well how to compose your picture it will also seem a natural thing seen in a great mirror.

Leonardo da Vinci

IL LIBRO DELL'ARTE
(OR THE APPRENTICE'S MISTRESS)

HERE BEGINS THE BOOK OF THE ART, MADE AND COM-
POSED BY GIOVANNA, IN THE REVERENCE OF GOD,
AND THE VIRGIN MARY, and of St. Eustachius, and of St. Francis,
and of St. John the Baptist, and St. Anthony of Padua, and generally
of all the saints of God, and in the reverence of Giotto, of Taddeo, and
of Agnolo the master of Cennino, and of Cennino the master of
Lorenzo, and of Lorenzo the master of myself Giovanna -------, and
for the utility and good and advantage of those who would aspire to
attain perfection in the Arts that they might know what lies before
them, and not be rash or unconsidered in their aspirations.

OF LAYING GROUNDS FOR PICTURES

Ottavo di Dicembre, this millequattrocento trenta-sette, a sur-
vey of the property: wide variety of trees: almond, fig and olive;
lindens, poplars, willows, walnut, maple, chestnut, peach and pear. Birds
perch on the branches; closer scrutiny reveals how mixed their breed
as well: doves and geese, hens and ... vultures; it hardly seems a recipe
for harmony; chickens, rabbits, white rather than black hogs, minevers,
a pond of fish. There is not sufficient order to imply breeding, farm-
ing, harvesting or gardening; the land, however, is not idle. An axe lies
on the ground.

And then a house: a rustic one, perhaps a barn, some structure
that appears to have been partially burned down, and through the inadvertent aperture whose scorched edges permit you to peer in, you
observe its squalor. The property outside is not arrested at the doorway—in that sense it is more barn than house—for it extends into the
vast interior. No one keeps the animals from strutting in and out: the
chickens, calves, the hogs and sheep—their jaws in constant motion
under roof as well as sky—roam freely. The minivers retreat, as is their

custom: this inverse greeting is your only sign of welcome. Rabbits, even fish (inside a pond and out) sometimes come into view; they leap, they hop, they stop, the latter flap upon a table or the floor as if they strove to swim in air. This is well, you think, for you are hungry, having traveled who can say how great a distance. And yet, alas, no evidence of cook or feast (although the air is redolent of garlic, most pleasant of its smells); no hint of special treatment toward the man who might as easily be friend as foe or stranger; in any case, your unannounced arrival remains unacknowledged.

You have heard of this house: that people also, though less frequently, less abundantly, wander in and out in curious attire, sometimes in scant attire. It is said that a woman relieves herself in the same manner as the animals, crouching on the floor. What sort of domicile, then, is this? Admit you're curious. Particularly when you spy whom you assume to be the very woman of these rumors, a handsome woman, of unusual appearance, striking, one might say, white apron skirts tucked up above her knees, as she squats over what appears to be not chamber pot but porringer, one of hundreds, you would guess, whose contents, after being baptized by this golden stream, are vigorously mixed with a skewer you had failed to notice in her hand. It is herself whom she addresses, when she sighs, "My private gilding." Then a pause. "But was that the proper sequence? Where are my instructions?"

The woman covers this concoction matter-of-factly with a white handkerchief, sets it aside, then seeks a pencil and scribbles something. Unfazed by someone's sudden presence, or her own awkward circumstance, she then addresses you:

"Welcome to our house," and then with raised voice she turns toward another corner, surely not to speak to sheep or hog, "No master, it is not your master, thank the Lord," before continuing sotto voce, "though in truth I would not recognize him." Then directed once again toward you, "and please excuse its sorry countenance. It is a curious property, I grant you, who stand outside the portal and gaze tentatively, with an expression I can't precisely read: disapproval, trepidation, mere curiosity perhaps? Or pure disgust? Earnest maid I am I must reply, when you inquire, yes, it is always thus, or nearly always. But not resulting from indifference, I assure you, quite the opposite; I will endeavor to explain, if time permits."

She moves from porringer to porringer, stirring, peering, pouring, and transporting; spanning greater distances, it seems, than those from house to house or town to town, greater than the distance you traversed to get here from a place that seems already a distant memory. She voyages with anxious animated grace, stepping over piles of rocks and dung, bones and feathers, limbs of humans—plaster surely—limbs of trees, sparring creatures, lolling creatures, bathing themselves with their tongues. And in the farthest corner, is one giving birth? As you're squinting to determine whether your interpretation is correct, or the misapprehension of numerous objects and bodies in disconcerting proximity, she addresses you again directly in ostensible non sequitur: "Can you tell me the weather, good sir? Che tempo fa? You stand out and I in, you have come from afar; I'm ashamed to admit I have no time to gauge the constitution of the day, for amid this abundance, only time is scarce. There is little room for chatting in our lives, nor for reflecting either, for that is what the gold must do, and we are but its handmaiden, as far as I discern, from what my master tells me, or what my master's master tells my master: he, inside, who serves this other unrelenting mentor, would greet you but he is always occupied." (as are the seats, you see, plentiful but unavailable for weary travelers; they serve as pedestals for pipkins, porringers, creatures, feathers, implements, all manner of sundry materials).

"Giovanna, do you call to me?" "No master, do not interrupt your preparations."

To my distinguished master, Cennino Cennini, on this day ottavo di Dicembre, 1437

In honestly and thoroughly reporting to you my progress, I must confess to you an omission in the figure casting of the prince and bishop both. The fact is, master, I neglected to add rose water when I washed the reddened bodies after casting; thus the noble fragrance was not part of either man's experience. Please bear in mind, master, that never having previously been cast, they will have no comparison, and neither will think less of us for the fragrance he is not aware he should have smelled. And, per fortuna, neither will offer to the other conflicting details, for each serves to mirror to the other my mistake.
Your persevering apprentice,
Lorenzo

"The house is more a studio, a workshop you might say, not the sort of domicile a man and wife inhabit, not the sort of house to which you are accustomed, but a grand disorder that will ultimately yield perfection for the glory of our Creator, who, my master, were he present, would not hesitate to remind you, also fashioned our world in a sequence, one day at a time. Although our Lord was thus engaged for but a week, and designed within his schedule a segment of repose. Of this I might remind my master."

Just watching, listening, makes you yearn for rest yourself, not from the residue of journey but from this energetic spectacle devoid of intermission.

"Master will soon summon me, for we conduct experiments throughout the day, at every hour, often night as well. No, he is not my lover, your raised eyebrow seeks an answer: our routine is indeed domestic but not conjugal; please heed the finger at my lips and let this be our secret, for a woman has her pride; you understand.

"Stillness, repose: time not to do—mio Dio, if only doing could one day be done—I was incorrect to indicate we lacked only this. Add to the list any quantity of love; what stirs the heart we have no leisure to indulge, while stirring all the formulae you see before you. Every day a color to be made, or two, or three; various kinds of glue, from lime, from cheese, from rabbit skin; I'm beating every shade of egg yolk and tending to their mixtures with more care than this poor chicken takes to make the egg that is their precursor"—she gestures toward the creature who now sits, domesticated, in her lap—"though I venture if she ceased to lay for us, my master's master would prescribe a way to make ourselves a simulacrum—which would, in fact, make my work easier, as I would no longer need to scurry between studio and town, where I find the hens who lay a lighter color egg, required by master when he paints the cool flesh tint of a young person's face"—idly stroking the annoying squawking creature, she at one point proffers you her hand, first fist, then loosely cupped, then palm flat out before her to display a new-laid egg! "This will be golden, nearly red", as if she could see through the shell, "but those from town a paler yellow, much less rich a color... it would be simpler to sit on them myself, until they hatch, but I am tending an infinity, if you permit my metaphor for these congeries of artistic gestation, and would ideally be, like God, in every place at once." Indeed, in this brief while, you have witnessed numerous activities involving animal and vegetable and mineral: stroking and cajoling; plucking and chopping; peeling, slicing, stoking, in general averting the disaster that seems to be every moment implicit in this multitudinous operation.

"If it be blasphemy to look on heaven, may we at least regard the heavenless sky? There I shall boldly seek additional recipes: a hummingbird's velocity, combined with the beehive's industry. We need to borrow from our earthly creature's wings to paint an angel's: wings and haloes both. If the chemist extracts color and medicinal substance from the insect, so should I be permitted to make a model of them in my mind: covet their flight and speed, while making do myself with feet, until they ache, until I'm out of breath, until my face is blue, but I confide to you my master's face is red if I refer, even in passing, to how an egg is made."

"Giovanna, to whom do you speak?"
"To myself, Lorenzo, memorizing, do not be concerned."
"He must not be distracted. My master, you see, has no time for love, at least he does perceive it thus. Conducting our experiments takes all his time—and by extension mine;—and making note of our results—at least those tasks which we complete—still longer. He feels compelled to keep a log of all we do so that his master, no longer looking over him, can be informed. Or so Giovanna does surmise. He sits writing to his master as we speak.

"In addition to my other tasks, I could deliver, were I permitted, master's missives to his master; he claims they are incomplete, and I say, should you not then finish one so as to free your mind to start another? (poco a poco finché tutto è aposto?) instead of juggling many works in progress, as we are required by circumstance to do in this our workshop, with our formulae and artifacts? Conversely, with your words, I've counseled him, you might move in a more reasonable, expedient manner, yes—be spared the overwhelmedness that one can't help but feel when confronted with..." —she gestures theatrically with her graceful golden-downed forearm, toward the entire contents of the workshop to indicate what words cannot translate. "At this point in our discussion he says that he 'will say no more on the subject,' a tactic of evasion he has learned from his master who often concludes instructions thus. His missives also must be perfect, I suppose, though I do not see how a gilded surface could shine as brightly when translated into words. I cannot help but think the time he spends with pen and parchment—since he remains ever in medias res—could be more immediately useful spent with me. Consistent work in tandem would surely add to our efficiency, allowing us to enjoy the luxury of an occasional siesta or the leisure to invite, and greet, the occasional guest, to show appropriate hospitality.

"For example, you arrived here at an awkward moment—although in truth there is no other kind within this six years' time—the recipe for the mordant required a quantity of urine. I do not stand on ceremony in master's studio, and thus I squat when necessary, fully aware that what is appropriate here may not beyond these boundaries constitute una bella figura. And thus, sir, lest you be misled by these motions of forming batter into loaves which I perform before you now, I am not baking bread, but making gesso grosso, gesso sottile, not wheat and yeast but plaster, water: that which coats my hands most of the day—and the tub to which you cast your eye, is not to shed the traveler's dust from your weary skin; the plaster must be kept therein until it nearly rots so as to get the silky texture we so prize; in the meantime, there are hundreds of things on the fire—and I, Giovanna, keeper of the flame—but none among them destined for conventional consumption; nor are any of these items the ingredients for the two light meals per day allotted to my master, whose voice you can, with effort, overhear, if you take advantage of those moments when the animals are relatively quiet."

Indeed the space resembles an inferno, a parody of perfection, not heaven but hell: a thousand fires. But how could hell be heaven's mirror?

OF COLOR AND PIGMENT

From some recessed alcove, a voice reciting as in prayer: "Sinopia, cinabrese, amatisto, dragon's blood, lac; ochre, giallorino, orpiment, saffron, arzica; verdeterra, verdigris, azurro..." He makes a canon of the colors, ending only to begin again.

"When I speak to master of what he cannot bear to hear, of love, or blood, secretions, freedom or the future, he recites to me this litany of lovely color words which do not rhyme, I am afraid, with mine, which were when I began a sweetest music, and now are merely numbers and relations; measures and motions: those which can be used in fresco, those which can be used in secco; all of the former, in fact, apply to the latter, but orpiment, vermilion, azurite, red lead, white lead, verdigris and lac cannot be used for fresco. More strangely still, no extraneous color is allotted to a woman's skin, says master's master; she dare not redden her complexion or her lips, for if she be so bold, her skin will wither on the spot, and the white of her teeth turn black, as will the beautiful blue of the painted Virgin's painted mantle if varnished prematurely. And yet in gilding, it is black under gold which makes the brightest gold of all, to reflect all the light away from your eyes."

Your eyes, meanwhile, are led away from her compelling visage to the unsorted storehouse of her stage. Her enchanting presence holds you captive no less than the clutter that confines you to restricted areas.

WHAT YOU MUSTN'T STEP ON (OR BUMP INTO):

Ten paces to the right a porringer, then another, a pipkin, a set of various sizes, furnaces, animal skins, furs hanging beside hammers, chisels; to the left and center, animal droppings of various kinds, plaster limbs: hands, legs and arms, can it be to the rear a dead body?, mortar and pestle, another of marble, dust everywhere, every imaginable tool, from pincer to axe, my God the stench, the chaos of aromas (now that you're beyond the threshold, tentatively projecting inward into chaos), fruit and flower and feces; egg and oil and garlic; a general putrescence difficult to define; brushes, bristles, handles, feathers, charcoal sticks, hare's foot?—goat's feet too, with skin and sinew—yes, they need good luck, you think; she sees you pick it up, says, "no, it's for disseminating precious dust. Did you think we were superstitious? On the contrary, we are practical; we are rational God fearing people (unlike the vain women of Firenze who according to my master worship their reflections rather than the one in whose image they are made) " —- next to the parchment and lead stile, you could swear you see a piece of bread; how hungry you've been; she sees you fasten your gaze and shakes her finger as if to say 'no, not to eat.' It is not an optical illusion, for this is really bread (rather than waterlogged loaves of gesso or glue) beside bottles of oil (linseed, olive) a marble slab, porphyry, with its quartz shimmer, a knife, bones of all sizes in various stages of imposed decomposition, baking dish, lamp, tubs, cakes, a basin, a penknife, scissors, brick, wax; no rhyme or reason to this vast desultory still life. Do you imagine vultures swooping over plaster limbs?

To Cennino Cennini on this day ottavo di Dicembre, 1437

Master, as to my progress, the report as promised. Yesterday I took a fish from the sea, to make a noble cast of it. Elated by my catch I thought to double my artistic yield, and trapped as well a bird that rested momentarily in flight, but I confess I had forgotten that living creatures without souls resist the process, and were expressly disrecommended by you. I could not keep them still. I did not wish to harm them. I thought, O foolish creatures, how can it be that you protest an opportunity for immortality? Later I realized these poor lesser creatures lack the soul that houses immortality, and could not have the merest understanding of art's glory. Sometimes the volume of my efforts overwhelms me and I err, I become careless. I painted 100 saints heads circled by a hundred glories as practice, or penance for my foolishness. I finally cast both bird and fish when they ceased to breath but lost much valuable time. And added, I regret, to their suffering.

Your rueful apprentice,
Lorenzo

What goes on here? You're walking on eggshells no matter which way you turn: pipkins with yolks, pipkins with whites, in combination with Lord knows what other substances; when spilled they make the floor's inadvertent varnish, which, once under your shoes, spreads everywhere. The house is like a hatchery, or bakery that produces neither sweets nor bread; yes, better to linger in the doorway than attempt an ambulant relation to this organic clutter. Alternating with other excretions are the eggs; they're everywhere. "Please find a seat if you are weary; I've no idea how long you've traveled." (The preternatural richness of her voice.) But easier said than done, as your gracious hostess is too preoccupied to realize what you've long ago discerned: that all the seats are occupied by objects. And she before you in another corner tapping egg after egg, balancing the severed shell to cradle that which it protected, draining off the fluid which surrounds each golden halo. "O Master," she whispers, not intending you to hear, "If only I could reveal to you of what I am reminded by the whites." She, mesmerized by this ostensibly mundane activity, also mesmerizes whom would watch. Thus you, in turn, without volition, inadvertent mimic, grasp an egg yourself; there are so many.

"But if I give way to reverie, I will forget my cataloguing, let me see, already I confuse myself: a half-baked mordant here; beside a nearly finished glue, a color on its way to... O don't drop that egg"—but too late, you feel a caught thief and a clumsy one; "no one of them expendable though numerous, I admit. O my, the minerver bit you," she exclaims, compassionate but distracted, you suppress your own alarm at the gratuitous attack of the same animal who fled from you when you arrived; "They are normally so timid, I'm astonished, sir, perhaps you provoked it? Mi Dispiace. These same substances from which we fashion color, are used by the chemist to make unguent and salve? But here where we have every formula in process, none among them is for healing that which ails the body. Madonna! What you've started here: the pig fights with the lamb, the basket of eggs overturned. I will need to make a second trip to town now. Mio Dio, is the porringer on fire in the pipkin? The flame was not supposed to reach it; now another part of the wall will burn, the wind will whip its way in and unsettle all our careful work... an infinite number of mixtures on the stove? And the sulfurous smell will linger, confuse me." How she fails to be offended by the general olfactory cacophony eludes you when the place combines the scent of barn, latrine, pharmacy, bakery, nursery.

"Che cosa, Giovanna? Do you help or hinder?"
"Master, while you sit reflecting, and I work alone, we can make little progress toward our six-year goal."
"I didn't mean to scold you, sir—our guest—or to imply in any way

you were at fault; It's you who may, instead, blame me, for this confusing swarm of things and creatures. It seems, I know, slovenly, but we are hardly indolent; you're trying to deduce what this plethora of props is for: a plethora of tasks that overwhelms even to itemize: we grind colors, boil down glues, (from lime, from cheese, from rabbit's skin); on which stove did I leave it? I must reduce it to a half... hence my boiling now, and then dry it in the wind, but not the sun—- How is the weather, did you say, or did I ask you, sir? Fa brutto, fa bello? Che colore ha il cielo? Pioggia o sole? Would you be so kind as to return outside to give me a definitive report? If my master finds me engaged in conversation, I am certain he would not consider it a wise use of time, not productive in the more apparent manner of making gesso, laying ground on pictures, working in relief, smoothing the surface of the plane, gilding, coloring, adorning with mordants—which I must attend to and upon which I must pee, or have I done that already? Ah sì, mi ricordo, our introduction: as you perhaps observed and thought peculiar (I have lost perspective). We paint cloths of gold, we paint also on walls, we draw, all this and a great deal more we do, and will continue to, for the next five years and nine months: insomma, duecento settantacinque giorni to arrive at a total of six years.

"Once a week I ask my master, on the eve of what I would, were I directress here, allow as day of rest—that which even our Heavenly Father observed—if when these six years time is spent, we might be something more akin to man and wife, or man and mistress—I in truth care not which; my humble upbringing did not emphasize distinctions of this kind. My master is devoted to his work, he is as assiduous as any man the Lord created, and I in my assisting him, mean fully to enhance his capability as well as to address what he neglects: his manly, human needs."

Transfer your attention to the large piece of fabric draped in the corner. Guardi. Senta. Two figures in white: "una domanda" says one to the other, mouths sensuous numbers: "uno, due, tre, quattro, cinque, sei; on the seventh day, master, may we make... love?; a lavoro finito, Lorenzo, amore?" and the second figure, perplexed, and far from playful, earnestly replies,
      "Dimmi, Giovanna, what service could I be, to mistress or to wife, when my daily duties occupy me thoroughly as these?"

Then she, naively, "But could you not perform, Lorenzo, drawing and your coloring, gessoing and varnishing, gilding and your tempera, according to a pace you yourself set? Must you learn simultaneously every skill in such detail"?

"Which then would you have me eliminate? I must know how to work with glue and fasten cloth on panel. And if I have the wherewithal to prime with chalk, but lack the skill to smooth the surface of the picture ground, how then can I go on to polish it? If I favor using bole to making gesso, I am surely incomplete, and any worthy artisan will tell you burnishing and gilding in themselves could take the practice of a lifetime."

"Perhaps then, that should be your task, to choose one expertise among these crafts and concentrate your energies, be known throughout the world!"

"O lady Giovanna, it is simply not conducted thus among the artisans; my master would not have it, for all these labors are related by their nature, and to understand the whole necessitates the study of each part."

"Lorenzo, may I ask, are you then but a mirror for your master?"

"Giovanna, are you but a hindrance to your own? Have I not told you every interruption, every conversation, is attention thieved from art, and energy that would be better spent producing? There is, as you yourself observed, a great deal to accomplish on our agenda. Have I yet mentioned tempering colors and laying on flat ones? Powdering a drawing, scraping and engraving, to rule lines, to adorn and varnish pictures..."

"O Lorenzo, I am enervated even as I listen. If only we could lie together in repose." The figures draped in white arrange themselves accordingly. The sun will rouse them soon enough. Suspend the counting sheep—and pigs, and chicken, minevers, for that matter, porringers—until tomorrow. ("Al meno fino all'alba, Lorenzo, stai tranquillo.")

Aren't you bold to pull back the curtain: a cloth of gold? Shame on you, what do you expect to find? An artist's workshop is no place for titillation! Would you seek to watch their breathing as they sleep? Your consolation prize: a sand-colored cloud: an entire flock of moths in flight! (Just as well to interrupt their gnawing of the now nearly denuded fur of the minever pencil someone remembered to bake but neglected to protect with clay.) There is so very much to look after.

And suddenly she's there again, before you, as if to scold you for your curiosity, as if she'd put a decoy in your path, and now resumes, at dawn, the day, without a pause. "May I suggest to you, O goodly stranger, that what you see before you is deceptive; you or I don't see as artists do" (she is presumptuous—if she only knew) but she links you, verbally, to herself, proving, you assume, she holds no grudge, "as my master does; for example, you see farm animals, and assume I am a dairy maid; you see a fig tree in our yard and think I tend a garden for its beauty or its bounty; when in truth the milky juice of that most sensual fruit is here gratuitous, irrelevant to its tender shoots required for tempera, and mere appendage to the woody trunk, from which we cut our panels and to one of which I one time lent my spit. You see fur pelts hanging from the doorway and assume them to be for my adornment and my warmth. But sir, I am no woman of luxury, for my father was a man of modest means. I play none of these aforementioned roles. Rather, I am apprentice to my master, who sees, when you and I see white or black, a range we cannot fathom, distinguishes a black made from the tendrils of young shoots of the vine, from a black of the skins of almonds, from the black of the kernels of peaches, and the most distinctive black of all, that which lies under gold, my master has schooled me to know, is the brightest of blacks and begets the most brilliant of golds."

And even she, Giovanna, unschooled until this time, in art and craft, can recognize the most singular black of her most grotesque imaginings, the black her teeth will turn if she adorns herself against his master's rules; in tandem with her withered face; it seems absurd, it is extreme, it must be gross exaggeration, but such a poignant, captivating face, if not conventionally attractive, does Giovanna have; her father called it pretty, and she prefers her teeth remain akin if not to pearls to chalk, to plaster, but never, Lord forbid, to part her lips for smiling, laughing, tasting, asking something of her master, only to reveal two rows of almond skins, or peach kernels; no, the teeth must remain closer to biacca, to sangiovanni, and her face, whether rouged or not, be smooth and fine, like the silk of gesso sottile. She has learned much since she began this post, but all the time is haste and fretting, labor and exhaustion, until at last the black of night offers brief respite, in which she places her impassioned fantasy of white— whose complement in day occurs each time she makes a formula with egg yolk, and separates the viscous white surround; she cannot help but think then of the first task she performed for him, his strange request: her spittle smeared on hardest wood.

To Cennino Cennini del Colle on this day ottavo di Dicembre, mille-quattrocento trentasette

I beg you, honored master, to consider my request to take on an assistant, in this expanded separate territory. I am embarrassed to admit that without your eyes nearby I am less prone to blunder, as my wish to please you is immense. I do realize I make an unorthodox request; please remember this would be a temporary arrangement only. I am aware that as apprentice, I am meant to do all duties, be indus-trious, improve my skills, increase my productivity, complete all tasks you set, but I feel my frustrations impede my progress, and per-haps with assistance, temporary assistance, I could learn by the example of one who stands in relation to myself as I to you. I could approach your standards, that is to say. Thank you, master for your consideration.
P.S. If you like, we could make a date in the future for you to visit, and determine whether I have by that time made sufficient progress to merit an apprentice, if you deem me worthy of assistance. Granting my request requires no effort on your part, as I have in mind a suitable apprentice.

Determined to instruct you now, she carries on: "My point, O pen-sive stranger, is only this: What we see as nourishment or sustenance, moreover succulence, what we take between our lips to put against our tongue and suck or crack between our teeth to rend from tough exterior an oily, savory essence meant to please the palate, is, in these quarters, something meant to serve the eye, which focuses all other senses, toward a far greater glory. In sum, my master sacrifices life to make all manner of work to please the eye, for others' eyes to gaze upon, and thus to obtain a love through indirection. My master conse-

quently has no time to gaze on me; and thus I would be interested to
see if he would notice were I, in consequence of indulging in cosmetics,
as forbidden by the dictates of his master, to wither as his master warns
a woman would—that is, my visage—or were I to open up my mouth
to answer him one day and spit, from toothless gums, a shower of blackened pits in lieu of words."

"Giovanna, do you monitor the sun for me? Can gilding be conducted yet?"

Sotto voce—"Had I asked of the weather, kind sir, a gray day, a
fair? These mutations occur frequently; each inquiry might legitimately
receive a different answer."

"But if our gilding is postponed, it is instead the most perfect of
all colors, upon which we embark: ultramarine to clothe Maria
Virginie, not to be confused with azurro della Magna, a color of great
merit itself, but lesser in comparison. The color of Our Lady's mantle is always blue, as clear a sum as one plus one is always unambiguous;
the room for variation lies within the blue itself; how rich, how luminous, how splendorous, and this responsibility, if she can meet the
challenge, is in the hands of Giovanna on this day: ottavo di Dicembre,
mille quattrocento trenta-sette. But why, she thinks, could the color
not be red?— since the Virgin's birth occurred to give the world its
special child: Her whole life since girlhood set aside for the sake of
an offering of monthly blood to ready Her to bear, in secret, the
flesh that housed His sacred saving blood.

"I suppose I can console myself to think of that humility, and have
a hope for my own possibilities, as distant as they seem; but children
here, can you imagine, stranger? I've too much to attend to, and during these six years when all other women's wombs bear fruit, I will elect
to be engaged in other creativity.

"These animals, per esempio, are like children, i miei bambini"—
she coos at those within arm's reach and actually nestles them against
her breast—"always needing minding, always trying to drink our formulae, eat from the precious porringers' contents. If only they would
leave alone the porringers, the recipes can so easily be ruined, and they
made ill, and they have not sense to make their mess outside (as you
have noticed, amusing how your fingers make a clothespin for your
nose, sir). The sheep, so used to grazing, chew whatever comes to hand,
to mouth, their jaw in motion morn and evening; sir, you surely see

a woman occupied in this peculiar fashion has too much to bear to bear a child.

"And yet I need to entertain myself, for it is a dry speech, you see, this following of instructions, this sharing of ingredients and formulae, not a normal discourse, no play in it, no heart in it, no feeling, and so perhaps I chat too readily, too hungrily, with you, who happened here quite by accident, and whose ordinary hunger, I, poor hostess, have not means to satisfy, as bread is here reserved for the erasure of the pencil's errors. For what would rub away mistakes if our bellies housed the bread? If I indulge your appetite it will, in effect, perpetuate imperfection.

"Per piacere, I began to speak of color and I strayed. My master has no doubt decided to postpone our gilding until later, absorbed in what he writes; thus I can start my principal activity. Today is the Virgin's feast day, for whom we make blue, because She will be painted by my master in her mantle. We, who have as our objective perfection, must focus our attention on this noblest of colors, according to the master of my master (though in my own attempts to make it I've begun to find it less entrancing, truth be told). Our Lord who made the sky, which is, I assume, our template, would be disturbed at such a clumsy, labored synthesis. Nonetheless it is the companion of gold in its glory; we gild day after day in honor of the moon and stars which occupy the midnight sky, whereas if we were truly God: one stroke and we exist; if there need be a thousand steps to perfection, then what is beauty worth? But it is not my place to question, and even doubt cannot hinder my devotion or my application. What greater proof of this than the fact that I myself have quarried this lapis lazuli in the mountains to the west—the mountains my master makes a picture of with those rocks behind the chickens as his model—with the least ashes available, as instructed; I was very careful to distinguish between this (ultramarine) and azurro della Magna. And now I pound it in this bronze mortar, then grind it on the porphyry slab not allowing myself to be distracted and hence delayed by noting the beauty of quartz against lapis, like a kind of star, and then I sift it through this special covered strainer—such as one might use for spices, in the course of normal cooking, such as did my mother for my father:

another procedure, sir, entirely—and then pound again. I must not make it too fine, or the intensity of color will diminish. Now for each pound of lapis, I must add six ounces of pine resin, three ounces glue, three ounces new wax—which if my master had extracted from his own ears might facilitate our communication, as calling back and forth above the din of this peculiar domicile is ill-served by additional impediments—all of which I have measured in advance. "And now? They must all be melted together in a new pipkin. Then they must be strained through a piece of linen which according to my master I am fortunate to find, as he implied I was profligate with it when I bled in menses. ('We have so little linen, Giovanna, he complains, to serve our art. You must replenish all supplies.') He thinks perhaps I should arrest the flow that makes me woman, to fashion a disguise from inside out in case his master comes to call and finds his unlicensed apprentice is mis-sexed. Allora, where was I: through linen, si, into this glazed basin, to which I'll add a pound of the lapis powder, mixing it well to make a paste, keeping my hands moist with the linseed oil. I must stir it every day for three days and nights, and keep it fifteen days or thirty days. After which time, the azure can be extracted. Then I shall take the two sticks, a foot long, rounded at the end and polished, with handle neither too thick nor thin as written by the master of my master. Then I will add from the original glazed porringer the paste to a porringer full of lye, which I will have prepared, and heated to be moderately warm, and then with the two sticks, I will mix it with one stick in each hand, emulating the manner of kneading bread, such as I once did with my mother in the house of my father, such as occurs in normal households, that are not consigned to making art—bread such as we rarely eat in this house. When it appears to be perfectly blue, I will pour it from the glazed basin into another, adding more lye. When this in turn is intensely blue, I will pour it in yet another basin, continuing on until the hue is tinged with color. And then, can you guess? I must dispose of it. Good for nothing, says my master.

"Però, non è finita! Then I must place in order the basins on a table, and beginning at the first I must stir up the azure with my hand, which will have sunk down by its weight to the basin's bottom. The first-drawn extracts are best, the first porringer always better than the second. And then it shall be for me to decide how many shades of azure I would have: three or six or what? If for instance, there are eighteen basins of extract, and I'd wish to make three of azure, the contents of the six basins are mixed together, to make one shade. The azure from the first two extracts is worth eight ducats an ounce. But the last two extracts are worse than ashes, despite the fact that the lapis I procured had hardly any ash. Daily it shall be necessary to remove the lye, that the azure be dry. When it is dry, I'll put it into purses made of skins, bladders, of animals I myself slaughtered, I who was thought by my father to be a squeamish girl, turning my head from blood.

"All this then, for what precedes the painting of a picture, sir. Is it not wondrous? Or perhaps ludicrous, I can't decide? I pray I have not revealed too much, but you can hardly be competitor to us, for if you were yourself apprentice to a master elsewhere, you would not have had the leisure to linger here. I must memorize through song and rhyme and recitation, so as to make less dry his master's intricate recipes, so intricate that no one could commit to memory from a single hearing: my master needn't fear. Devoid of narrative the tedium does haunt me."

"Giovanna, to whom do you now speak?"
"A beggar sir, who when he sees what we provide prefers perhaps to go without, and begs no more."

"But you, sir, never utter, you gaze intently at me and all of my surround, just barely blinking, your pupils marching back and forth from left to right as if to find a linear way to catalogue this chaos; your nose offended, your ears assaulted; it is vertiginous, I grant you, you should seat yourself, collect yourself, and I will show you that which we collect, as I've no other hospitality to offer. You too might wish for stasis, not this process all exploded but a dainty single image with quadrangled boundaries politely offering itself for focus. But when you watched me make the ultramarine, I hope you felt a certain soothing meditative quality, methodical, sequential; it may in retrospect collect you, as I always pray, it will do me. How you happened upon this house I have no notion, but I imagine it is not what you expected. And this unites us, stranger, for I too had no inkling of the life I took upon myself.

"In point of fact, sir as I labor, measuring and mixing, I find myself wishing my master could imbibe the blue of evening's sky, the gold of the sun, even the gold of which my hair would seem to be spun; so said my mother, as she braided it for me before bedtime when I was young. 'You will make the girl conceited,' scolded father always; 'she will expect a spouse more grand than we can manage to provide with our modest dowry, lacking jewels; a bit of fabric, some preserves in crystal jars, at most one pig, two chickens'—it may not be apparent to you now, sir, as I need to pin it up and twist it round lest gesso coat it, soil it, or lest a carefully crafted angel's nimbus appear to unravel before the viewer's eye because my strands' inadvertent contribution rested where it ought not. For in this workshop we use strokes as delicate as hair; and the brushes that we use are made of finest animal hair to make the whirl cascading down a painted woman's back, but if some part of me infected this, it would be tainted. Illusion of strictest imitation must not collide with the ungainliness of flesh and blood.

"And yet flesh is something more than word; flesh is other, is it not so, stranger? Master, for example, has no manual for my menses, and thus cannot accommodate, cannot adjust our schedule. He shades vermilion with fine lac to make with paint the drops that mark a dead man. And the holy blood of Jesu Christo is revered. But dragon's blood and lac to me suggest an imagery definitively womanly. If you'll excuse my frankness, sir, the pipkins I could fill with what spills from inside of me, one quarter of each moon, as if eggs were also breaking there, within my womb, an egg with color even darker than those cultivated here, so gold inside as to be red, as these tarocchi oranges we in Toscana and Lazio and Sicilia so prize, those rubied fruit would stain a linen more than I, and no one turns from them. In my humble opinion I think dragon's blood no more exotic for a color than a woman's blood, yet no color is attributed to her, sir, in our quite extensive palette. Non importa, I would have no energy to do so, filling pipkins far too frequently already, sir, including on those days each month that hinder my efficiency, and thus don't please my master, though his reticence about the matter inhibits true discussion, just as once when we were fashioning a painted cloth of gold to make a woman's petticoat, I thought his stammering and awkwardness preceded some most unsavory admission, such as my dismissal, or some complaint about my person or my manner, untidiness or such; in truth I thought he was about to say, my menses interfered too much with my abilities as apprentice. I will never know what master sought to tell me then, something related to a letter he had finally finished, I felt the weight of it, but if I prod him now he is steadfast in his refusal, says he "will say no more on the subject" although the subject is as yet undeclared. In any case, I can tell he thinks on numerous occasions he has made a great mistake in endorsing my apprenticeship. His discipline exceeds mine by mille bracci. Not even Sundays does he rest, not even feast days of our Lord which were, in my upbringing, never questioned.

"But perhaps after his six years, all the accumulated Sundays and feast days and week days can be ours, because I, Giovanna, do think I could easily lie with my master for six consecutive years, in strictest sequenced symmetry to these of toil, thus to have reward and work in equal measure, while he would study, with my good assistance, techniques his master did not encourage him to learn; and we too would think it appropriate on Domenica, Lunedì, Martedì, etc; tutti i festivi et tutti i feriali to pursue a craft whose manual we might together write, in an ink almost transparent, in an ink resembling that more liquid part of the chicken's egg not favored for our working formulae and we would likewise be occupied constantly by our leisure, pursuing that postponed art with alacrity and diligence, crafting day by day and night by night.

"Allora, all very well for me to weave my fantasy, for drudgery invites reverie: Giovanna's cardinal rule, and it is human nature, I believe. But were the master, I mean master's master, to appear, here, in our midst, as close to me as you now stand, there would be nothing short of mayhem because a female would not likely be appointed to my post, and a mistress is, I fear, forbidden; thus what disguise could I possibly acquire?: neither helper nor whore—and do not think I haven't schemed, sir—to protect my master's dignity and allow me to remain here in this household, this workshop, as his assistant in this curious amorphous space. There is no place for me, a woman.

"Unless I be but form, unless I do not move, and be content to find reflection in a mirror master makes in paint or plaster, unless I cease to breathe, sir, like that man there behind the furthest pipkin about whom I would beg you not to draw conclusions.

"You, understandably, see all manner of sharp tools nearby this wounded man, and assume them weapons. Those tools, however, did not make those wounds, but recreate them elsewhere on a surface that could serve as mirror. Insomma, that man serves as still life; the world and all of God's creation one vast still life, awaiting its depiction; and all that grows wild or cultivated, all that is concocted and assimilated upon this property: each is merely one ingredient toward achievement of perfection, for which the soul is instrument of measure, but the eye is ever mediator."

"Giovanna, a chi parli?"

"Nessuno, Lorenzo, a me stessa."

"Non domenticare Giovanna, I am the safeguard of my master's secrets, his formulae, his intricate techniques; I pray you be conservative in your speech. You must be circumspect. Ti prego."

Now whispering not to you, but to the first reluctant, then aggressive miniver, who does not shun its mistress's lap, as she strokes her cheek against its fur, "Miniver, would my master care what else besides his master's precious secrets I might give away?"

She begins, the animal still in her lap, to pile all items in her immediate purview into groups more uniform than any you have thus far witnessed, forgetting entirely for the first time, your presence? Eventually you realize each thing between you now occurs in groups of six.

INVENTORY

from chickens, eggs which in turn make gesso, their bones to grind and fire for priming.

from calf and lamb, parchment.

from rabbits, their skin for glue.

from minivers, their fur for brushes.

from birds, (geese and vultures) their quills in which to insert the fur bristles of the miniver; feathers to smooth away error (or stroke lightly her pleasure when master is not watching her discreet dilatory gestures).

"Stai tranquilla, creature, do not protest, it is only a single bristle plucked, you should by now be well accustomed, you will disturb my master; come now, goose, your honking is excessive, a single feather does not diminish you, O do lie still."

from olives and linseed, their oil.

from fish, their innards for glue, their bones to grind for priming, and their form entire for casting. from hogs, the white better than the black, their bristles for brushes. from poplar, willow, linden, fig tree, wood panels upon which to draw. also from the willow, sticks to make charcoal. Containers and vessels for all that is created: bottles and pipkins and porringers; casseroles, bowls and jars and tubs and dishes. Scissors, penknife, hammer, chisel, wire, axe .... Eccetera

Pull back the curtain. But do not be seen. A woman and man, both clad in white. He's weary from lack of sleep, and she whispers as they stir, his hand on hers, perhaps the fifteenth porringer this evening, "Master, will you promise me one thing, please promise me that when the last of these ...tasks is done, you'll put your hand, with equal ardor, on this form which you have often cast, I should say tried to cast." She looks out into the area behind this small enclosure with her enormous fawn-colored eyes, likewise glazed with fatigue, which has the effect of making them appear to protrude even more than usual, as she makes ready to retire: "Lorenzo, anch'io, sono stanca."

"We are not here in the habit of enumerating sheep to aid our path to sleep but for our weekly inventory, no matter how sleepy we might in counting find ourselves to be; we don't indulge our weariness as we take record of our raw materials: we catalogue our flora and our fauna; our subjects and our objects; our models; our both animate and still lives in this vast warehouse where life is seldom still on its tumultuous trajectory to utter peace and harmony; paradoxically there's precious little poetry on the way to art, and our exhaustion serves as antidote to the insomnia that might lead those in normal beds in normal households such as I imagined as a child—to use this child's device, a formula so innocent, to move from day to dream: uno due tre, quattro cinque sei, poi subito a dormire. Shorn or no it matters not; they only need appear, and before long a child hears bleating that lulls him, that pulls him into sleep. O would that I could pull the wool over my master's eyes, for when he is weary I sense he becomes susceptible to my suggestions, surrenders all defenses, all his fortresses of color to dream in richest black and white.

"You, stranger, with no model for the single-mindedness and devotion you perceive in me might find inside your mind some box to put me in called category: a clinging or a doting or a nagging wife, perhaps demented in degree of my resolve. But I am none of these as much as volunteer apprentice, though I could not say precisely, yet, what I expect to learn. Nor should you assume I carry out my master's bidding uncritically, unquestioning, for we do argue, at least discuss, as he does never, to my knowledge, with his master. Perhaps you think that latter model more worthy: unexamined emulation. But how could I, in female form as my soul finds itself to be, be mirror of the space between my master and his master? I would do better to adapt the tasks I find as I cannot adapt what Dio has made as me. This is not a woman's role, then, your raised eyebrow denotes, but I would ask you why a woman unencumbered by a husband or a child could not devote some portion of her time to a most worthy cause. I wield an axe as well as any man, with practice: these varnished panels against the far wall prove me true. As to immodesty of modeling, I am certain that has crossed your mind; may I be frank: if this is meant to glorify our Lady, I suppose I'd just as soon disrobe my person as to take the veil. You must remember that an artist sees with more refinement than do you or I, sir; quindi, you'd serve me well to lower your eyes, sir, if you intend to stay throughout this coming session, when the figure casting starts; it is a most complex endeavor, in some ways harder still than gilding, for again, we never finish, as my master lacks apprentice while I am model, and chi sa? Perhaps my master so loathes the imperfection of the disproportionate female body that he cannot bear to complete the task, for he invariably runs before the greasing is completed, to "relieve himself", he says, and does not heed me when I urge him to do just as you saw me when you first arrived, to contribute to the making of our mordants. On the contrary, he flees, declaring 'I'll say no more upon the subject.'

"Once when we had run low on oil, for I had yet to milk the olives of their liquid, I said, 'master, could you not, in emergency, grease me with another substance?' 'But there is no alternative, for we have run out of linseed oil as well, Giovanna.' 'Can we not then be resourceful, master,' I had asked, 'carry on beyond the book and be, in truest sense, creative?' Perhaps I had allowed the two supplies to diminish simultaneously; perhaps I put both bottles in an unfamiliar place. Was that so great a sin? I had not meant to thwart but rather to enrich routine. There is alas no danger my disrobing will distract my master. In general no sooner have I done so than he seems perplexed, becomes intent instead on gilding, and must be reminded that the weather is a factor in our ability to carry out that task."

OF GIILDING

To Cennini del Colle on this day, ottavo di Dicembre, 1437

Master, believe that I've become a better craftsman since my last attempts. But gilding continues to elude me. I concur it is the highest challenge, as you have indicated. I beg you to forgive me the wrinkle in the gold leaf, the less than perfectly smooth surface. I confess I sought, only in wish and not in deed, the company of woman, but one woman, and in my mind's eye only master, on the night before the gilding. And how my trembling hand betrayed me, just as you had predicted; but master, understand, this was the result of mere imagining (perhaps because I, Lorenzo, maker of images, know the power of picture, sometimes greater than what is represented.) The very image of her shuddering under me creates my yearned-for, heaving pleasure, and leads me to declare that no artisan in Italy, indeed in all the world, could ever craft a surface smooth or lovely as her infinitely tender flesh, that I confess when I have touched within the needs of my profession only, I also longed to linger in for other purpose. O master, when in my dreaming (during the meager sleep my labors offer) she was spent in my arms, I was blinded to the brilliance of this metal and its quest for immortality. At these times six years seems indeed eternity, until apprenticeship is through, and then, I would assume, I shall be encouraged to use my own judgment; I can dictate what serves well or ill my art.

"Scusi, stranger, the weather? Note for me, if you would, its demeanor, for if it is windy but not sunny I can set the glue to dry, and if it remains cloudy we can resume our ever-interrupted gilding, alternate activity to our ever-interrupted figure casting, which is not contingent on the shift of cloud and sun as much as the mysterious mercurial constitution of my master.

"Do you not find it fitting, sir, that gilding be conducted under canopy of cloud? For if the sun graced the sky, would it not mock the gold which we produce in emulation? I do not wonder it retreats (to our advantage, technically). Nonetheless, we remain apprehensive lest it reemerge, and carry on with caution. Sometimes I feel I do no more than go through the motions of our gilding, since we seldom advance further than the preparations, and peccato, you are unlikely to witness my master in the actual act, but I can visualize all the steps from the few times we have executed them to completion, and as I practice enumerating them you may through your imagination see the esoteric process.

"Thus for my master, I lay the panel flat on two trussels, which I have taken pains to secure away from the chickens and the white pigs, whose motion and whose racket might disrupt this most important process. I shoo them inside if they come near, to do Lord knows what mischief to all our other dormant preparations. And I pass my feather, by which I do not allow myself to be distracted, over the panel, then the raffietto after, to discern any roughness, any knot. If there are no knots to be removed, I burnish with coarse linen the bole, and at this point, he, Lorenzo my master, brings the tooth which I myself cannot claim to have extracted from the lion. Better that it be in his possession than mine, as I might idly stroke with it my skin and even without asking I know my master would consider this highly inappropriate, for it is even more important for the burnishing of gold than bole, this tooth, and necessary to us, as we are not of sufficient means to use, in lieu of such, a ruby, sapphire, emerald, or topaz; for a man devoted to his craft has no time to make profit in this life, and a girl of modest dowry such as I cannot offer jewels: a country girl from Arezzo, as I mentioned, not Firenze, where the lips and cheeks of women are as much akin to rubies as the jewels I imagine to comprise their ample dowries.

"Once cleaned and burnished, I put for him into a nearly full glass the egg white tempera and mix it thoroughly with water, (and its frothing causes me to reflect upon another image which I promptly, dutifully banish) and then with the pencil of the miniver's tail, those fine hairs, which I myself preserved in clay to keep away moths, I wet the bole, holding the pencil in my right hand, while he in his right hand takes with the pincers the fine gold to lay on the square card, somewhat larger and turned up at each corner.

"He wets the bole equally, so that no part has more water on it than another, and then taking great care not to wet the card, he releases the gold, and as soon as it has touched the wet part, he snatches back the card, because now it has become part of the panel itself. When my master sees, however, that some of the gold has not adhered to the panel, I offer him a piece of the clean cotton with which I stand ready, so that he can gently press it down, but I can see that he is anxious lest the precious substance go to waste and he need to start again all over. In this manner he is to gild the other parts of the panel, and before he lays the second piece of this finest thinnest golden stuff, he wets the panel, trying not to wet the first piece he has just laid down, but he is clumsy with the fur tipped pencil of the minever, and wets what he should not and we must begin anew, and how I wish I could soothe him in a way my instincts tell me, but instead I must give him only the brick-sized cushion covered in fine soft leather, such as might comprise the boots of a gentleman of Florence, and on this he rests the remaining strips of gold, which will adhere to the handle of the minever pencil once it has been wet with his lips and which if he would ask me I would myself wet, as I did the cuttle bones for priming on that first day and which I am tempted to take, after he has done so, discreetly, into my own mouth.

"It is always my task to supply the giornata, for there would be no point in laying more gold on the surface than can be burnished in a day, although we are so often interrupted by the sun or other intruders (not you, sir, of course, I mean not people but circumstances, creatures, exigencies of our particular ambiguous household) that excess is rarely a problem. It pains me to see my master err, for I have seen him succeed as well, and he is admirable in dexterity and concentration. When having begun again from the first step, he does succeed in joining the two gold strips or pieces by breathing from his mouth upon it. And when I witness this, I feel covetous of that substance for reasons far more esoteric than its preciousness or permanence. And then the sun, which we are often pleased to see and in my childhood I would always welcome, interrupts again our labors, we cover all with a clean handkerchief (again it seems to me in humility or penance for our hubris) and choose among the hundreds of lesser activities on our agenda."

"Perché non è mai finita, questa cosa, Giovanna?"
"Non è mia culpa, ma il sole, giusto?"
"Non so, ma vorresti aiutarmi?"
"Sì, per sei, ma non per sette, dieci o settant'anni."

It is inevitable that there be occasional irritability between master and apprentice. It is as clear a sum as one plus one, or orpiment plus ultramarine makes green, that disappointment following anticipation yields frustration which in turn creates a wish to blame, which soon enough evaporates, under sun or under cloud; for there is far too much to do to indulge pettiness or bickering.

"But when we burnish gold laid not on panel but on even surfaces, we do so with a piece of lapis amatisto, warmed and felt to make sure no powder lies under it, as one feels powder between one's teeth, (those who have not lost their teeth to vanity) and if so it is swept (the gold) with minever tail. The gold is burnished gradually, first one side then the other, and its surface should be smooth as a looking glass, such as might be used by the haughty heathen women of Firenze who love their beauty more than God, who think their own reflection good as gold. I wonder, stranger, might the mirror crack if they smiled in satisfaction, showing two dainty rows of blackened pits? Might it break, to make a jagged outline such as that which you peered through initially to see this circus of a workshop, and be less easily mended than the gold, which is repaired with another piece of itself lain over it and breathed upon, and then burnished immediately? When properly burnished the gold will appear brown, from its own brightness.

To Cennini del Colle, on this day, ottavo di Dicembre, 1437

Master, yesterday I took the bird that screeches at me night and day; the one that you've bid me ignore and I confronted it; wrestled with my own hand til that screeching ceased. O cock that crows at dawn and dusk and sometimes through the night, I had to write my own instructions for attending you. I sang her name in order to drown out the fowl's fury as he took flight. I revere my honored master, but he would make my song in flight into a dead fish. You warned me that my hand would shake were I to keep the company of women. On the contrary, from but thinking of her, its rhythm is more certain; its motion is deliberate and vibrant. Note well, dear master, this flapping fish that surfaces at every inconvenience will be no longer humble, nor be vulnerable to hook or net. The wish to glide, the wish to fly, now vies with my desire for perfection. I bid you note this detour.

"Persistent, patient, silent stranger, how uncomfortable to find yourself confronting what is already in progress, with no conclusion imminent. A species of explanation as to how this arrangement came about would be the minimum of hospitality. Perhaps you'd like to know how this began. (I suspect you may possess a nature curious as mine.) I knew Lorenzo from my father's trade, and once I had to bring a message to him when papa was ill. During that visit, I observed a greater disarray than what you now behold. Could I offer help, I asked him, for my mother raised me to be generous and industrious, and I shan't make you guess the nature of my master's first request to me. (Compassion was my impetus at first—then I realized I simply liked my master's company; he amuses me, so serious and earnest.) On that day he brought me bones, not of the chicken, but the cuttlefish: ground into fine dust, such as you and I, sir, shall become, rotting away to that which you see before you—-a thought by which perhaps you are made squeamish; though be consoled, the soul, of course, shall go to God, inviolate, while we, the we you see, shall wither worse than the women of Firenze damned to perish by means of mirrors as they foolishly favor the coloring of flesh instead of represented flesh."

DEAD MEN AND BONES, PISS AND SHIT, FIRE AND CHAOS, FRUIT AND FEATHERS, ROTTING MATTER EVERYWHERE, all on the path to putrescence, the path to milk from matter lasting beauty.

"Excuse my digression, sir, the bones, I had begun...that he had very finely ground and asked me, he asked me, pardon my giggling, my sighing; you must never tell him—this is deeply secret, sir—he asked if I would be so good as to take a half bean of the bone's ground dust and mix it with saliva. (I didn't know then the purpose: to prime the panel he would draw on) 'Whose saliva shall I utilize?' I asked him, as I knew he had many folia of instructions. 'I don't believe the source is specified,' said he, 'but I am certain that this is a less than refined act to ask a lady gracious as yourself.'

"'No, no' I protested, 'nothing that assists you is beneath me,' surprised by my own conviction, and pleased by his concern, 'it would please me to contribute to the honor of our Lady, and your drawing' (for I knew even then he consecrated all his works to our Lord and the Virgin). So I surrendered modesty and made the little bubble form from my pursed lips, to mingle with the dry dust of cuttle bones, this tiniest of alchemies; and he gently took his forefinger and rubbed with it the dampened spot my mouth had made, to spread the mixture all over the surface of the wooden panel which he held in his left hand. 'Please guide my finger too,' I requested of him, 'hold and move it in the appropriate motion.' Then emboldened in a fashion I would not disclose to everyone, to anyone, in fact, but you whom I will never see again, who has no consequence to master or myself, who seems in silence not to judge, 'what else,' I asked, 'might I prime for my master?' and found my finger at his lips or his at mine, I can't recall; it seemed the same, until he fled reciting every shade from blue to yellow, green to red. I feared my imminent dismissal, having only just been hired, and have numerous times since then regretted gestures of the sort, which I, alas, am past controlling. As clear as day they are improper here. Yet, even reason seems to buttress my assumptions. The animals, for instance, who share our house, think nothing strange in bathing with their own secretions.

"And in the manual I, Giovanna, aim, if ever time permits, to write, I will include what master's manual omits—questions such as this: if the body is creative, should not the artist who inhabits it be in equal measure creative, exploiting all resources, nothing wasted; nothing overlooked? I feel that I can say to you, a stranger, more straightforwardly than I can say to my retiring master: why piss and spit be privileged over other liquids? And why saliva in one's palm but not skin's other surfaces? And if man's body be the model of all beauty, and thus each man inherently correct in form, why not make that truth available to all concerned, at least to Giovanna, earnest eager diligent apprentice, who seeks to learn all that she can in as expedient a manner as possible?

"'Do you think it evenly distributed, good lady?' was the last question my master asked before I made transgression. (I speak still of our introduction.) 'My less than expert eyes would judge it so,' said I,' and that was the inception of this professional collaboration. I have performed many curious acts in only three month's time but none gratuitous, and I learn much. Oh, do excuse the hog who buts his snout against your leg; don't mind his grunting; he too is hungry; I must pluck more bristles from him for my master's pencils and it aggravates him; you can understand. He too prefers to be fed. I have only plucked the minever this week, whose tail I shall bake once the casserole of coals is removed from the stove. When did I place them there? He, the silly hog, seeks mischief, since I fenced the geese away from him. Their honking never ceases; they are worth less than their feathers. O to be a hen with a simple task of warming with her body what she lays, how singular, how sedentary, how salutary."

HONKING SNORTING, GRUNTING, CACKLING, BLEATING, COOING, SCRATCHING. How can a man think? How can anybody concentrate? Where can you take refuge? Why can't you remove yourself, as if instead of egg, your feet were lodged in glue?

Peer through the curtain. This golden cloth: a perfunctory gesture of modesty; like a veil of gossamer golden thread, revealing something between silhouette and flesh, a fresco come to life, between shadow and painting, fra chiaro et scuro: veiled figures who erect a wooden case, tall enough to embrace the one but not the other, figures from whom voices emanate:

"It surprises me your master bids you make a cast of female form, as he claims none are perfectly proportioned."

"It is so, Giovanna," replies the male apprentice; "only man in all his parts is measured justly. In woman there is greater variation, and thus no true standard. This is as the master lectures on the subject."

"But is it not strange, Lorenzo," the female challenges, "that in all the world there be not one, not even one breadth of shoulder, width of hip, one curve of breast or calf or span of hand that might be, by pure accident or indeed divine design, formed in just relation?"

Giovanna is admittedly not proportionate in strictest symmetry, the breasts grander than the hips, the left of the former not precisely the equal of the right, nor aureole either, once one looks more closely, as precision of depiction can demand, and suddenly this slight asymmetry intrigues Lorenzo and you who watch him watching. As if he'd finally found perspective (paradoxically through your hidden eyes) or seen it for the first time truly, as she, his model and apprentice, enters the tall wooden case built to the height of a man's chin, with the templet of copper adhering but not pressing against her skin. In a way, her nose conjures the beak of a bird, while the lovely nearly bulbous eyes a fish; it's all askew, one out of scale with the other but somehow pleasing, yes, intriguing, against the plaited golden hair, itself like ripe wheat in sunlight, like gold foil under moonlight; Lorenzo is not a poet; he is a painter, draftsman, craftsman. He needs time to fashion words, requires quill and parchment. Patience.

"My master (he must struggle to keep his composure) would refute the very possibility, Giovanna, but I imagine even he, were he to see, for instance, evidence, set as it were, in stone, in plaster..."

"Or in flesh," she interrupts him? "what if proof in very flesh?" — -she holds his hand against her.

"He, my master, would never be, as artist, so stubborn, as to disbelieve the truth before his eyes."

The apprentice continues her interrogation: "And how would truth in such an instance find him?"

"Allora, if such proof somewhere on God's earth existed, I would consider it my duty to display it."

"Less simple a matter than to display to God, whose eye sees all, whereas your master only sees what would be put in front of him?"

He makes ready to pour the plaster front and back, but how can he, without the help of his assistant, pour both simultaneously?

"But master, do display for me the evidence that would support your master's bias. What better opportunity shall there be? Moreover, how can I learn without such tools as would persuade me intellectually, through reason and through demonstration. Otherwise this theory remains for me an abstraction."

"This theory, Giovanna, is merely a matter of measure. Master teaches that the body of man can be measured in faces: one from navel to thigh; two from thigh to knee..."

"In that case, I could take my face against these measures that your master dictates, as you hardly could contort yourself in such a manner, to illuminate me."

"Shall I grease you, woman, lest this plaster harden long before we begin to cast? Have you placed the olive oil within my reach this time?"

She turns clandestinely to you, who thought yourself well hidden. "His eyes, it seems, do scan my parts with admiration. Could you afford me objectivity, O stranger?" (You are embarrassed to be discovered.) "Do I deceive myself, do you suppose? Do I read as his desire my own? Of course you could not see his eyes as I had bid you cast down yours?" Discouraged for a moment only, she carries on with him who tries to cast her.

"Is it then erroneous, Lorenzo, that all the creatures fashioned by our Lord, in his own image, are innately perfect?"

"In essence it is so, that we inherit the Lord's perfection in what resembles him, but the ideal beauty of the artist has as his vocation this: to craft a beauty visible as aid to beauty spiritual. But we must interrupt our discourse to begin the casting; speaking will be difficult as I begin to cast the face."

"But of the figure casting, master? Yet again postponed?"

"No, il viso oggi. Your face so near me casues.."

"Master, causes?"

"... so near inspires in me the necessary ....to do the far more difficult casting... of the face. Il corpo a domani."

"Master..."

"Basta."

"Master, would you make of six years seven, ten or seventy?"

"Madonna, Giovanna, do you help or hinder?"

There is only occasional irritability between apprentice and master; who are not, after all, engaged in competition, altercation, but benign cooperation, yet when under pressure of long hours and unrelenting labor, anticipation preceding disappointment is as guaranteed a recipe as any color in their repertory.

"Va bene, Master, as I will be henceforth indisposed, I cannot serve you in the usual manner, so you must work independently."

"Esatto, Giovanna. The first step, I know without regarding my instructions, is to shave the beard with the razor in my right hand."

"When casting MAN, master, not a woman; feel how smooth a woman's face is." Through the gold veil, she places his hand against her cheek. "I think it better to practice such steps as can be practiced on a woman, while a woman lies before you. Therein lies reason."

"Hai ragione, Giovanna. If I can find my miniver pencil, I will then proceed to anoint the face with oil of roses."

"O dear master, how the fur-tipped pencil pleases my cheek and nose and chin as you stroke."

"Giovanna, it will be better when the plaster stills your tongue, for you distract your master. These techniques are not designed to be...responded to, capito? If you are ready, then, the cap on your head, and the band sewn around it. And then I insert into each ear this piece of cotton; tell me if I go too deep."

"O hardly master, you can press more forcefully (if you like)."

"Sewing is not my greatest skill, so this capuccio to your collar is askew. Without your assistance, it will be particularly difficult to place securely this hoop of iron, two fingers wide; do not be frightened of the saw-like teeth inside."

"On the contrary master, I find it fascinating every time."

"It may be unwieldy for me, but I shall take great care, don't fear, that it not touch your face."

"But you, if it would help you know the subject whom you cast, should feel at liberty to touch her face."

"We must not delay the placing of the two small silver tubes, light and like fingers, to fill perfectly each nostril."

"Then do insert them master, where you would. Sono pronta." Her master does so. His subject ceases speaking, and presently her skin begins to turn a blue that has little resemblance to azurro della Magna or ultramarine, a blue her master has not seen and has no reference for. A blue that comes from inside, and cannot be synthesized. But you, more worldly, watching, you have traveled, observed with objectivity the world in its variety. You can immediately identify the problem, and feel compelled—you cannot help yourself—to solve it. He (or someone) failed to pierce them like a trumpet, to allow for respiration. The subject simply cannot breathe. Thus the golden-tressed apprentice faints away, but fortunately lands on piles of fur and feathers, instead of fire. Six chickens squawk in unison; six eggs release six liquid suns, six pipkins tumble.... "Per la mia vita, put your mouth on mine." You hear a phrase that noone said, yet in a timbre rich as cream or yolk of egg, lodged, intractably in your head, as if instructions from a place beyond your own volition. In this emergency you have an obligation to draw back the cloth and enter; the circumstance demands your interference. You have witnessed, silent, long enough.

To my valued apprentice, Lorenzo, on this day, tredicesimo di Dicembre, il millequattrocento trentasette.

I will henceforth have a new apprentice in my studio; thus there is no need for you to return there. You may continue to work in your separate structure, if it please you, or you may apprentice yourself to a new master, but if you elect to do the former, and wish assistance, you must interview for a new "apprentice's apprentice." I realize we were only in the infancy of your own apprenticeship, but I have found, not a more worthy, Lorenzo, but a more suitable apprentice, quite by chance. For just as new chemical recipes for color come to us when we are otherwise engaged, precisely when we do not seek that thing which we discover, I have now found that openness to change is a necessary ingredient in the development of the artisan. It need not be widely disseminated at this time; I inform you only because you are directly affected. Complete revised instructions shall be forthcoming. Yes, the taking of action and a willingness to adapt, to change, even a certain impetuousness in certain instances: these shall be prized qualities, which may surprise you. Your disobedience, incidentally, need not be punished. There is no more to say on the subject. Nor need you send whatever correspondence may have accumulated in my absence, as it would very likely be irrelevant. Buona fortuna.

Cennino Cennini

IL LIBRO DELL'ARTE (TREATISE ON PAINTING)

Here again begins the book of the art, made and composed by Giovanna -------—in the reverence of God, and the Virgin Mary, and of St. Eustachius, and of St. Francis, and of St. John the Baptist, and St. Anthony of Padua, and generally all the saints of God, and in the reverence of Giotto, of Taddeo, and of Agnolo the master of Cennino, and of Cennino the master of myself, Giovanna, and for the utility and good and advantage of those who would aspire to attain perfection in the Arts, that they might know what lies before them, and not be rash or unconsidered in their aspirations...

THE SPECTACLE

ACT I: WHAT IS A HUMAN

The human is a curious animal, characterized by a constant nervous motion. This one, for instance, stands on his hands and turns as if to make himself a wheel; the spokes that are his arms and legs intend to blind me as he spins. If I lash out in my confusion, he seeks protection in a wooden barrel and rolls before me thus contained. Or if I am about to take a part of him inside my jaws, or grasp him in my paws, to make him just for one moment still, then he leaps away into the well, or else takes some tall pole to spring to where I can't reach.

When he himself is not in motion, he waves before me reeds or straw, or this revolving wooden object which when I strike to stop it, makes the audience around me sound a music that is not unlike my roar.

ACT II: WHAT IS IDENTITY

In the center of this enormous oval space, the venator, no sooner has he met the lion, merges form: his shoulder with its face, and all the rest of him intact. His arm has been consumed, is what we initially believe, but if we'd gotten to our seats in time, we'd know the fierceness of his gesture. We too would have been startled to observe the stolen moment when the beast's jaws opened up to yawn, to roar, that gesture interrupted by an arm plunged down its throat. Now the venator, with the other hand, of his still visible arm, seizes the tender pink tongue; thus paralyzed, the beast's sharp teeth hold no peril.

The Emperor cheers, the Emperor seems to sigh. The Emperor shivers, holds his side, as if by magic, disappears.

I had not meant to swallow this strange projectile, that forced its way into my mouth, and chokes me now, while the only mobile part is gripped with his other hand, strangled by his fist. I do not like the taste of what encloses me: this adversary who assaults me in my most delicate cavity for the pleasure of the crowd. I am surrounded and invaded at once. Hear me, though I be an unexpected orator. More than my teeth and my roar; I too have softer parts. Often I've held the hare in my mouth so gently that it never felt my teeth's serrated edge. And here you, human, do the opposite, you strike instead of stroke. What could caress instead constricts; instead of bid me lick your salty palm, you bind my tongue, the way you bound my limbs when we were introduced far from this place. That was the first time, you'll recall, that you invaded my quite clearly designated space.

We cannot exit unobserved, as can the Emperor; he can choose to be invisible or prominent, depending on his moods, depending on his needs; at one moment brandishing his sword to slay some arbitrary animal, at another slithering down his marble steps to regain his composure or relieve himself, or observe the ones observing.

ACT III: WHAT IS INTIMACY

The panther and the bull address each other; the distance between them equal to the length of the chain that binds them. They lunge, exchanging mass and speed. But when they try to flee from one another, they are forcibly reminded of what weds them. Who is better suited as the victor: he with teeth or he with horns? The more massive? The more lithe? Sometimes there are answers, ladies and gentlemen, numbers bear out certain patterns, but for the most part nothing is for certain. This is why you're here: to witness the results of the circumstances we've contrived.

ACT IV: MAN AND BEAST

He grips my neck with his knees and when I buck he squeezes all the harder; by my motion and by his grip we try to make a victory, locked together like enemies whose kiss is fierce, whose kiss addicts.

He must desire his prominence. Because of the processions which use us in great numbers; because of the togas all the humans gathered here are wearing; because of the special seat he occupies, the wider for his comfort.

ACT V: WHAT IS INTIMACY

No one is fooled by it, neither of the participants certainly. They know this is for the stage's sake, that he with his gold-dusted mane after prancing regally to greet his adversary, stands perfectly still, arching his back, thrusting forward his head, offering his cheek to receive the lips of his partner, the same who might have caught him unsuspecting during yawn or roar, this venator instead glances his face against the beast's so softly, his own cheek titillated by the delicate slender filaments no human face possesses, at this moment the only vestige of cage's bars between their forms.

ACT VI: WHAT IS LEVITY

Did you see the chariot making a figure eight around the amphitheater?

How elegantly it delineates, how perfectly precise. The driver is so clever, yes?

The driver, did you notice, darling, is an ape! Those poor wretches in the rafters never get the joke, they can't see that far.

Sea lions, all present, bark to their respective names, as the Emperor calls attendance: Vespasian, Hadrian, Maximinian. He's named them after predecessors, how the Emperor is amused by their antics and his own clever joke, so amused he feels stitches in his side and will excuse himself before too long.

But what can stitch a rent flesh mantle, a gaping wide enough to expose all internal organs?

And what if there were nothing to cling to but the smooth marble that allows no grip; its slick voluptuous surface, making humans slip and slip and slip until they find themselves inside a pit of those whom they have gathered for their pleasure: the circumstance their criminals encounter.

OVERHEARD
The elephant is kneeling, do you see?

The dwarf must have ordered him to, just like last time. The games, you see, become redundant after years. It takes so much wealth and whimsy to make them always more exciting. Perhaps it's just as well to be in these less coveted seats, leaves more to the imagination. Just as now you imagined the dwarf; he isn't here this time. Then why is the elephant kneeling, you fool. He looks like a baby first learning to crawl.

If all of you weren't separated by protective moats and scaffolding and nets that obstruct even the closest view, you'd be able to see the single javelin between each toe of the elephant's foot: metal flowers humans planted. You think he has such thick skin he cannot even feel. Indeed the crowd thinks this a charming skit, some brilliant sacerdotal wit: an elephant who genuflects before his adversaries, then comes begging for their mercy. But ladies and gentlemen, there's no mercy to be had. If you stop laughing and keep looking, looking closely at the scene that is before you and much more than it appears, you'll observe this massive beast even thus reduced come charging, directly toward his foes, juggling shields as he goes, and straight toward us, oh my. And this I can assure you is not written in the script. He has intention to obliterate.

INTERMISSION

The glories of human engineering designed this stadium, this stage, these props, these protective measures and this ritual. Do not dare discredit the overwhelming grandeur of human engineering, whose transport took you across the sea and gave your life a purpose, to let you be a part of the most improbable, impressive of all spectacles.

ACT VII: WHAT IS MERCY

The creature who never forgets knows that humans remember. He is contrite, now, as he kneels before the Emperor, not so much the worse for wear for the bruises inflicted by the rhinoceros he killed, admittedly provoked by flaming darts to goad him. Before he was annihilated, the rhino threw a bear into the air and killed a bull as well. Will elephant be pardoned? There's no telling; mercy here is arbitrary.

For instance the deer, behind him, next in line, who kneels before the Emperor seeking supplication—or a momentary staying of the hounds that chase her—might receive a pardon, or she might receive two arrows in her head to simulate the horns she'd sport were she the stronger male.

IMPROVISATION

And the Emperor, who has been made a fool of by this massive interruption and is perhaps tired of being focal only in the audience, takes center stage, so no one can mistake his presence. He takes the role of gladiator, venator, and with his crescent sword, locates the longest neck of all performers present: even the slaves, even the women in the rafters could have guessed it would be ostrich. One can hear their collective sigh from the top tier, at what one would presume is hardly visible, but the Emperor, standing, arm raised, possesses better than a front row view of the exotic bird, one of three hundred who paraded for him earlier. Her vermilion tinted feathers now sport more than festive decoration, as her uncrowned trunk gallops back and forth unnavigated. Scooping up the ball that was the head and lifting high in front of him the stained, gleaming sword, the Emperor finds the senators' box—perhaps the ones who crossed him in assembly— and brandishes his trophies, as if to say: you could be next.

It does not disorient the Emperor to perform; he is accustomed to display, and is not bothered by the crowds he has assembled to observe us, and can choose at any moment to retire.

But what if the Emperor's open mouth, when cheering, yawning, what if it, like the lion's, were violated, while he gasped for air? Would the outcry of the crowd be deafening? Or would what sounds like outrage be in fact resounding cheer?

ACT VIII: MAN AND BEAST

Elevated from the bowels of the amphitheater arrives the lion in his box. A door clamps shut behind him, while the door before him opens to expose him to the crowd, and to the man, who stands without a weapon, probably a criminal. The former can't retreat; the latter can't defend himself. This won't take long.

But when paw and palm come together, touch is catalyst: remember that sharp thorn that only the dexterity of grasping fingers could remove? Can animals feel gratitude?

ACT IX: WHAT IS MEMORY

The audience's eye cannot help but follow the severed head, now tossed away by the human who's lost interest in it. We thrust our intact necks and strain our ears before the oddest sight: a tiger nuzzling it, possibly trying to heal with his tongue, in a gesture of unscripted tenderness. Stationary for the longest time, is he attempting to communicate with it, or listening? Tell us tiger, what you hear: give us one of memory's voices.

I had never felt it before: the sensation of being held like that, enveloped, protected, not since I was inside my mother's egg. My soft plump body in human arms so much kinder than ropes. I am special, getting special treatment, I am fondled, and indulged. Our legs work together and he is careful never to place his shod foot on my two toes. He is leading me, I thought, he's teaching me the way that humans dance—though human had been until then a foreign species—clutching a wing in his hand to give me balance and steady my gait. My long legs, I thought, at last were matched, by our equal heights, despite sinuous deviations, for he was straight where I would curve, so sometimes his chest brushed against my throat.

Venator, take this prop away, it makes the Emperor squeamish now. Why else would he be rushing to his seat? Is this too brutal for his gentle eyes: the act that he himself performed? The Emperor for all his ostentation is occasionally a bit withdrawn. He virtually melts away into the crowd, blending subtly in his seat, like an animal who has received from nature the privilege of camouflage—although it's true, the Emperor's enemies cannot hide from him. But what rises now under the tunic of the Emperor? Where is his other hand, which usually conducts the spectacle like an orchestra of carnage? The curtain of his tunic subtly rises from the pressure of this surreptitious magic wand.

ACT X: WHAT IS DELICACY

Not since Vespasian's day have we seen so much of the elephant, that once rare performer, who has appeared twice already this afternoon, and more often than not on his knees. His colleagues carry him now on a palanquin, as if he were a pregnant woman. Then one dances while the other smashes cymbals to make music. He appears to do a pirouette as she takes her place at the banquet table he's jut set. How daintily he pats the ludicrous pink skirt as he sits his bulk upon the bench with delicacy beyond a human's capability. If there is the least displacement, if one plate or vessel is disturbed, he coils it in his trunk to place it elsewhere with great care. And when the banquet is complete, she becomes scribe, and scratches with an implement on paper. Show your lessons to the Emperor, how the Greek and Latin characters are formed as by an artist's hand. But make certain what you say is what your tutor showed you. παν γαρ ερπτον πληγη νεμεται "Every creature is driven to pasture with a blow?" That can't be right. Fortunately, it's growing dark.

ACT XI: WHAT IS EROS

And the lion in the twilight shadows takes the hare between his jaws. He's running off with his prey, we, watching, think, but look how the hare's ears and legs extend as gracefully as a dancer's limbs, and notice that he does not yelp at all. Should he so much as twitch, the former, stronger one immediately adjusts his transport. For from the corner of his eye, the lion who makes his mouth both carriage and cradle slackens still more the tension of his jaw. He will not rest until each time he gently scoops the smaller creature, he can truly make his tongue its bed.

And I say to the vestal lady beside me, Imperial woman though I am, with every privilege, including this proximity, this coveted closeness to all aspects of the spectacle of which few women can boast, I cannot help but harbor secrets, wishes, such as this: O that my husband could cradle me so tenderly when my essence rests inside his mouth.

ACT XII: WHAT IS GRAVITY

There is no spotlight, only moon, by whose illumination we can fortunately see a single figure, bulky though he be, perform gymnastics and then dance. When all other creatures sleep, and humans too, he instead repeats a gesture many times: stand, leap roll; one, two, three, he does not miss a beat, and then rises, puts one leg aloft to find a slender rope suspended, and I can scarcely believe my eyes, he walks across it, though the bottoms of his feet are wide as saucers.

It's true, I can confirm, you do not dream, unless we dream in tandem: he climbs the proscenium in moonlight and balances himself upon the rope suspended many meters above the amphitheater floor. First he walked across the ground as if it were air instead of earth, each foot placed carefully and deftly, and then it seemed he turned the air to earth. Only when he finds himself across this precarious void, does he lay down his immense weary body, and rest, his breath slow, so we who think we may be sleeping, see its rise and fall.

We think we are dreaming him? We're only here because we've come the night before tomorrow's games to get a better seat, or any seat. We are poor, you see. We fasten our ragged cloaks with tarnished brooches and our gaping shoes the same. But we have had a gift today, that no one not forced to wait on line would have. Even the Emperor who sees so clearly from his unobstructed seat, whose width is greater for his comfort, whose podium allows him exit unobserved should be find himself bored, fatigued, aroused or squeamish, has not had this privilege of witnessing a dream behind the scenes: the animals' voluntary dress rehearsal, their own incessant practicing until perfect.

ACT XIII: WHAT IS EROS

The cranes now do their mating dance, chase each other round the amphitheater. The females prod the males; the males respond, or vice versa. They'll make a show of lust, appear to lose their heads lest they be taken literally, like ostrich. And in the midst of all their antics, the venator, perhaps eager for variety, seals his face to the tiger's in a gesture of affection. But the tiger is less cooperative than in the past. The beast is still distracted by the rolling ball now separate from the walking neck that carries forward frantic, unimpeded. It seems that he is coy, flirts with the lips that seek his cheek; the audience, enchanted, sees a mating dance between two species: man and beast. And finally their heads reside together, minutes it would seem, as if the tiger had confided something, as if he'd whispered in the hunter's ear:

As you trapped me do you recall the crystal ball you tossed upon the ground to furnish my diminutive reflection, so all that was maternal and protective in me thought I saw an embryo of my own flesh and blood, thought my cub lay trapped yet in my reach, so every instinct bid me lick to heal the poor abandoned newborn. But while my tongue made contact with the surprise of cold smooth surface I anticipated would be warm and yielding and familiar, you surprised me in much grander style. You closed in on me and I had no defenses. You kicked away your trick, your crystal ball and made me march.

Hastily the venator removes himself; it must be time to set the stage for closure, the grand finale.

ACT XIV: WHAT IS ALCHEMY

Even stranger than the mating dance of cranes is the gait of a human clothed in flame. It's surely better to be a citizen and wear a toga in honor of the Emperor, than to run ten meters in a toga that is specially constructed to erupt in flame, to earn one's daily bread. The clothing, then, that makes one civilized, can be illusion. And flesh can also be a cloak, as when physicians educate themselves in ways they can do nowhere else, to see so much exposed of what still breathes.

ACT XV: WHAT IS IDENTITY

As if the ocean overwhelmed the shore, the sandy amphitheater floor is inundated to make a giant oval pool, within which bulls and horses romp together, splashing, swimming, pulling boats behind them. A shepherd stands atop the grandest vehicle. A violent motion jerks away the hood atop his cloak to show this shepherd's whiskered face is not a human's, but a lion's.
Is it a trick of light? The Mediterranean sun dances on the sudden liquid skin of the arena. Gaze well, ladies and gentlemen. Gaze until the sun makes you squint to see beyond the surface shimmer. What you fix your gaze upon with indefatigable fascination is itself a kind of mirror. This oval frame contains a portrait you have painted. But there's no need to sign a portrait titled "Self."

6 *Chella ca guarda 'nterra* — Quella che guarda a terra	7 *'e Peccate* — i Peccati	8 *'a Mmaculata* — L'Immaculata	9 *'a Figliata* — la Figliolanza	10 *'o Cannone* — il Cannone
16 *'o Culo* — il Deretano	17 *'a disgrazia* — La Disgrazia	18 *'o Sango* — Il sangue	19 *San Giuseppe* — San Giuseppe	20 *'a Festa* — La festa
26 *'a Messa* — La Messa	27 *'o Cantaro* — Il pitale	28 *'e Zizze* — Le tette	29 *'o Pate d' 'e criature* — Il padre dei bambini	30 *'e palle d' 'o tenente* — Le palle del tenente
36 *'e Castagne* — Le castagne	37 *'o Monaco* — Il monaco	38 *'e Mazzate* — Le botte	39 *L'Acqua* — L'acqua	40 *'a Cumunione* — La comunione
46 *'a Pummarola* — Il pomodoro	47 *'o Muorto* — Il morto	48 *'o Muorto che parla* — Il morto che parla	49 *'o Piezzo 'e Carne* — Il pezzo di carne	50 *'o Pane* — Il pane
56 *'a Caruta* — La caduta	57 *'o Scartiello* — La gobba	58 *'o Sepolcro* — Il sepolcro	59 *'o Gallinaccio* — Il gallinaccio	60 *'o Sacramento* — Il sacramento
66 *'e figliole zitelle* — Le ragazze nubili	67 *'a Casa vecchia* — La casa vecchia	68 *'a Menesta* — La minestra	69 *'o Signore* — Il Signore	70 *'o Palazzo* — Il palazzo
76 *'a Funtana* — La fontana	77 *'e diavule* — I diavoli	78 *'a Femmena 'nfama* — La donna malvagia	79 *'o Mariuolo* — Il ladro	80 *'a Vocca* — La bocca
86 *'o Putecaro* — Il bottegaio	87 *'e Perucchie* — I pidocchi	88 *'e Casecavalle* — I caciocavalli	89 *'a Vecchia* — La vecchia	90 *'a Paura* — La paura

TOMBOLA

I

It is Christmas and the boy, with no thought of the old man he will become, is imagining instead what he wants for Christmas. He is not thinking of the spirit that needs no material gifts, the spirit his Mama says is the true meaning of Christmas, nor the chamber pot, he, infirm, might have by his bed at home or at hospital, in years to come. Least of all is he thinking of a death by another's malevolent hand, that death which lurks in the shadows, whispering rather than speaking. He is not even thinking of the woman on the balcony, opposite his family's terrace, who would send flowers for his funeral, the woman to whom he later, in his adolescence, will wish to send flowers (his adolescence, soon upon him, the stage between now and the old man he will, God willing, become, is far too remote to the shy, unpreoccupied boy, who doesn't realize he feels such feelings for her, that he is even capable of such feelings). He is far from considering himself the master of the house, whose blood might someday flow from an unnatural death. He is a boy who can fall off his bicycle and scrape his knee, a carefree young boy who stares laughing at the hunchback who passes by. For Christmas he wants a cat, and at this moment he is hungry for his soup.

At the age of fifteen, following his uncle, he arrived in a farm between San Cataldo and Marianopoli, in the countryside of Caltanissetta, where he was having an appointment with the chief. "After the reunion, in which I did not participate, the men went outside, they embraced me and kissed me and also gave me the money in their pockets. It was then Uncle Luigi explained to them that I had demonstrated I was destined to be affiliated with the organization."

II

There is something strange around the head of the Virgin Mary, something round and glowing, you are crazy, says his mother, have some coffee take communion, what, did you fall and see stars?, fall on your head with so little brains already there; brains in your culo; blows from the back of my hand will stir them up, then you should go straight to church like a good ragazzo instead of looking up a girl's skirt to see what looks always at the earth. Find instead a girl who could be your bride, Beppino, a good girl to take to church, take off your hat, Beppino, when you get there, always take your hat off in church, in the house, did you think you were living in a palace? If this is a palace then where are the guards? I would ask them to take you away, to the cave, to the grotto where you go to do what I know you do with the girl, when instead I might have had a child to whom the Immaculate appeared, a boy who would recognize what encircled her head as a holy accessory, not something from outer space.

Today, twenty two percent of Italians attend church on Sunday; a third or a quarter take communion, but only half of this number request confession.

III

Lord forgive us our sins. It is Christmas, we are on our way to Church, led by the landlord, said by some to be a thief, said by some to have two women, his tenants, so called, a decent and a wicked woman, both of whom, can you imagine, sit beside him in Church, on Christmas day. Both of whom parade up to take communion, and who quarrel, hands folded, one behind the other, on communion line, about the recipe for minestrone, which the honorable woman makes with more vegetables than beans, and the wicked woman makes with fagioli far outnumbering verdure. Whose soup he chooses is a stressful game, a test of love, and he has daily indigestion from the pressure of a choice by which he cannot win—compounded by the gas after he eats the spoils—for sometimes he runs back and forth from apartment to apartment, sipping, slurping, belching. I wouldn't be surprised if they all ate, together, less than one hour before receiving communion, gluttons that they are. Only those who stare at the poor devout hunchback don't stare at them in indignation or fascination. From the time the rooster crows, they quarrel, loud enough to be heard by the woman at the balcony across the way; the charming signorina is too gracious to complain, to shout "Basta" from the balcony, but this is Italia after all, and the landlord, sitting, kneeling, standing between the decent and the wicked woman, listening to the priest drone on about the joyous news of Natale, cannot dispel the image of the legs of Lily.

Certainly the temptations of the flesh always threaten poor mortals. Fornication, masturbation, adultery and homosexuality for the Church remain grave sins. Abortion and contraception are very grave. But the devil has assumed many new forms that put society in danger. Theft is a sin.

IV

I will beat you if you stare at the crazy man, says his mother, saddled already with a brood of children, or if you go out in the nasty weather without your hat. For dinner you will eat only bread, and be lucky to find a bride, if you continue to insist on using these naughty words, think of nothing but tits and ass, and Beppino, I gaze in astonishment at what was made of my own flesh and blood, that seems instead the work of devils. By the Lieutenant's balls, I don't know what to do with you. The death that speaks.

Confession was once an art. It has been said that Catholic countries weren't acquainted with psychoanalysis because they had confession. The bad action confessed unburdened the sinner of anguish and blame.

V

If I go to mass every day, Lord, might I be blessed with a baby girl, relief for all the stress I receive from my son, il mio ragazzo, and may she, la mia ragazza, remain a maiden until such time she finds the man to be the father of her children, such as my boy, I fear, already may not be fit to be; may she be a maiden, not a piece of meat such as might be peddled by a shopkeeper, one night surrendering her flower to some drunk. Have a good cry over the 33 years of Christ, I now am the age of our Lord when he was crucified, and I go from grotto to fountain to grave with the same sound of the same bird in my head.

Twenty years have passed since the time that armies of psychoanalysts and scholars decreed the death of the family, at any rate that danger. Today, instead, the exact same group of analysts reaffirm the validity. Why?

VI

There is blood in the garden. It does not come from under the signorina's skirt, that mysterious place which sees always the earth, nor from the sacrament. There is death and there is sudden senseless death by someone else's hand. But have a glass of wine, forget it, dream of the lovely mouth of the wicked woman, watch the Pulcinella skit. Pray to Saint Anthony for the mind you lost, and be grateful that you live in Italy. Buy some roasted chestnuts on the street, even though they cost, don't knock over the chamber pot so distracted are you by the image of her mouth. But what death makes sense? says that sensuous suddenly disquieting hole.

"Why did I leave the Mafia? The fault of Toto Riina, the head boss. He betrayed the rule of solidarity that I thought formed the basis of Cosa Nostra. He used two different standards. He followed with great interest the trials of the men closer to his heart, on the other hand he did not show the same interest in us, the others."

VII

With my hand I fire the canon, with my knife I eat my hat. Don't listen to me, I'm a fool. What's got into my head? The weather is bad. Send me to prison where I can have a good cry, and grow old, like the old woman who lives here where already I'm the master of the house, an old house, and your mother and I had you brood of kids instead of dancing around the fountain that we may as well turn off in this terrible weather.

They declare the death of the family, but in reality they are making a sort of artificial respiration that had in those years the effect of revitalizing.

VIII

If I lived in a palace, I wouldn't need to be a thief, I could live, in society's eyes like a monk, but sit dreaming all day of the breasts of the woman on the balcony, who someday if I were brave enough I would invite to a party, but I am too timid to be a good hunter. The soldiers who pass under the balcony never fail to garner smiles but I only from the hairy one. If she flew from her balcony to my palace like a bird I would crow like a rooster, present her with flowers, then later a boy, and if that's still not enough, a little baby girl. And yet it is death, in the end, that speaks.

The representation of the feminine was in fact from time to time affirming an idealized type, as in the "Italian woman" of the Renaissance, the "new woman" between two eras, the "woman of the new Italy," after World War I, the "new Italian woman" of fascism...

IX

I confess my sins to St. Anthony, and he seems to find them for me everywhere, devils in the garden, devils in the church, even if I have an innocent fleeting thought of the woman on the balcony after a glass of wine. I toast the soldiers who carouse by the fountain on Christmas, on their way to Church, where I also, father of children, go, eating roasted chestnuts well before I take the sacrament, of course. We must all take the sacrament because of the fall that preceded us, reminded of it even as we admire the lush interior of our church, bedecked with flowers. Would it be a sin to bring one back to the woman on the balcony, who if I were courageous I would ask to escort to midnight mass?

When I was giving confessions, I noticed many times the penitents wished a sin to confess but couldn't find one. They didn't have a notorious sin at their disposal, and supplied in general the missing of Sunday mass. The new catechism is useful for the confessor because it enlarges the list of sins, invests all of social life...the quotidian enters in the space of the sacred across less confessable moments.

X

Because of shed blood during a quarrel, a man of honor is in prison, whereas, the shed blood of a rooster or an eel would not put a hunter there. In prison praying to the Virgin or dreaming of the maidens whose buttocks can no longer be observed, and that part of her which always regards the ground, under her skirt, now unavailable, will make a fool of you. At this party there is only bread and cheese and imagine that!—the man of honor wants to flush himself down the toilet.

The account of Giuseppe Marchese, "soldier" of the family of Corso dei Mille of Palermo, threw a bit of light on the complicated arena of the Mafia: countless informants, massacres more and more ferocious, finally leaving a deep gorge in that rift between the upholding and the violation of codes of honor, in particular the side of "corleonesi" of Toto Riina, a group who executed violent acts...

XI

What is your fear? asks the monk of the hunchback. Is it old age? Is it woman? Woman is wicked, says the hunchback. Do you not desire a bride? I desire, says the hunchback, to shoot a baby out of a cannon. You could not then take communion, says the monk. I desire to rub my hump against the tits of a wicked woman, and then against the bride bedecked for betrothal at the altar. What has this to do with spirit? asks the monk. You began this story, retorts the hunchback; you taunt me, you know before I am old I cannot take a bride into the palace, whether or not she leaves her tits outside, or at the altar. My bride, says the monk, is the thirty-three years of Christ. This bulge in my back, bellows the hunchback, my poor excuse for what I cannot give my bride, and for what you hide grotesquely under your coarse, modest robe.

The Eastern Church sees correctly the confessor as a doctor rather than a judge of the spirit. In this perspective, the art of the confessor must be that of reminding all penitents of the possible sins, and then to make available to all absolution.

XII

His first communion, and even so there is a cannon in his head with tits and ass exploding, he can't help it, is he a pig then? That is what the woman whose T and A he fantasized would say, as would the old one or the shopkeeper or the hairy woman: all of them stingy, all of them in need of wine, or a sudden senseless death. Madonna! How holy he felt until that cannon went off in his head.

And how to reintroduce the sexual argument in confession? Strictness is not enough. I see with pleasure that the nightmare of the past, masturbation, is treated with new comprehension. Perhaps this is the way to understand in what sense masturbation and premarital sex must be confessed. Because people today don't ask for indulgence, they know themselves all too well to be guilty and are relieved to have identified just what it is they are guilty of.

XIII

The boy is being beaten because he is worse than a thief; he exchanged the chamber pot for the minestrone, and behaved like a hunter in my garden, took his hand to the bird, whose fall he claimed not to hear; he claims he was drunk but on what? On caffe? He is drunk on his fantasy of what of her regards always the ground but peccato, there is no hospital for what ails the spirit. With my hand I try to atone for the fall he represents.

"It is easier to speak of the more traditional sins. Blasphemy against God is in first place...The kids have greater attention to ecology, the ones who confess to have destroyed plants and mistreated animals."

XIV

A brood of children will make you soon enough crazy, a fool, or a wicked woman stuck in an old house because the bad weather never gets better. If I pray to St Anthony I will only find another baby and the master of the house will go into a stupor, to find he is again the father of children. St. Giuseppe, he will cry in his stupor, spare me the sacrament, I need only water, tomato, some bread.

At the end of an era in which she has become, with great effort, mistress of her own life, the woman closes the grand search traced from the pioneers of emancipation and feminism...If all is maintained she will not renounce one millimeter of the inherited victories, but she does not wish all she has gotten to be flattened to a condition of parity with the male. The actual difference is affirmed as women profess that the rediscovery of identity of family comes sanctioned by laws and by rights...

XV

The knife that cut eel and pork and cheese and tomato for the party is the same knife we found inscribed in his chest; can you explain that to your mother without fear of appearing a fool?, standing in your tie and tails, praying to the Virgin and St. Anthony to please God find you quick an explanation, shoot you quick from the cannon with two sacks of cheese roped around your neck as if you were a horse, shot like a comet, into the palace far beyond?

Cosa Nostra wasn't the group he thought, but only a criminal group, who convinced him to enter into a family of informants...Leonardo Messina began to speak profusely of himself and others, of the Mafia, of the structure in Sicily, in the rest of Italy, in foreign countries, clarifying that the summit is not that one known in Sicily, but that there exists a national and a world Mafia.

XVI

Fortunately the fall that led to his death came after he had taken the sacrament, the soldiers reported to the old woman who lives in the old house where she offered them caffe and they escaped from the hairy one, who always offered them nothing but water and chestnuts. On their way to see the Pulcinella skit they invoked San Giuseppe and why, they wondered, when they arrived, did the black-masked, white-clad commedia del'arte actor bow obsequiously from the stage and offer them his hand.

The Mafia is a particular case of a specific economic activity: it is an industry that produces, promotes and sells private protection.

XVII

The guards, were they supine, would be delighted to regard what regards always the ground, under her skirt, but not in front of the monk, because that would be a disgrace, as bad as being sent to prison, or becoming instantly an old man, to whom the mouth of a woman is memory. But the mouth of a woman, reflects one of the guards, is itself a kind of prison, both prison and garden, is it not? It is part of a person's head, after all, but not the same as the man's, is it? Not just a place to pour wine. The guard is a hunter of just such mouths, so sumptuous that they could cause men to be sent to or from a hospital and cause misers to fill their chamber pots with gold.

"The woman who thinks to emancipate herself imitating the

man refutes her natural procreative and educative mission, and with her very hands constructs a destiny of suffering," written in 1918, making many enemies, by Gina Lombroso...

XVIII

Since I'm not a monk but a fool, I can pray to St. Anthony for what I never had in the first place: a maiden to call my tomato, whose tits put me into this stupor. She could call me her rooster and I promise not to be a pig, I will offer her the eel I can now only hold in my hand, inspired, says the monk, by devils, but the monk and I often quarrel, as I would never do with my maiden who is more basic than bread; if only the saint would answer my prayers and tell me where she is hiding.

In a short time period she had to make haste and find a husband, or rather accept a husband, always the family's choice, making sure this arrangement occurred by the age of twenty-six, canonical of spinsterhood.

XIX

San Giuseppe would approve of the brood I produced, but I swear I would have done otherwise had I been a hunter, a shopkeeper, a thief (shooting or stealing or selling cheese), and not the drunk that I am. My brood and the bad woman whose mouth will be the death of me shall send me to the sepulcher; if I try to imagine the size of the lieutenant's balls I will weep, in my inebriated state, one tear for each of the 33 years Christ spent on this earth. The hairy one looks at me and I feel my years exceeded his already.

With our life expectancy touching upon 80 years, with a youth that is protracted until 40, with a child at the right time, in contrast with our first great great grandmothers, who in 1881 could hope for a life of 34 years, who were having at mid-life five children but saw two more babies die, who were "old" at 30....

XX

It's a disgrace to think of the legs of Lily when you are already the father of children, a new baby no less. (Go ahead, get as close to her legs as you want, they're as hairy as mine, and I bet they have lice.) The miser won't offer you wine in congratulations even as you stand in tie and tails, you will have to take water instead from the fountain. The baby's mother calls you a man of honor, and insists you leave the party, complimenting your handsome chestnuts, to go through wretched weather to receive the sacrament.

She had to learn how to wield the single power that her sex reserved her: maternity, making a weapon against mothers-in-law and brothers-in-law. Above all, she had to model her daughters on images and resemblances of values she herself had inherited.

XXI

When the mouth of the hunchback opens to receive the sacrament, you would think you were at a party rather than in a church, as if the Blessed Virgin herself fed chestnuts to an eel, as if a boy took the knife in a quarrel with the baby girl, his sister. As if a quarrel had erupted in our old house, into which no one but a man of honor is ever invited.

The person comes preselected by a man of honor, who studies at length his personality, his behavior, and the quality demonstrated in criminal actions such as theft, robbery, arson, etc. Only if there is already evidence with repeated and unequivocal attitudes the aspiration of entrance to the Mafia can ascend to the first level...

XXII

Would you trade the legs of Lily for the wicked woman's tits? Would you trade your sins for the 33 years of Christ? (He did for you, ungrateful wretch; you call yourself a Christian?...) Would you take the old woman as your bride, rather than the woman at the balcony who you have yet to get to speak to? Are you crazy? The blood of those 33 years for your sins, and all you can do is act like a Pulcinella on the stage, you're too old to be spanked, your punishment, we've decided, is death, go to your grave.

At this point the man of honor asks the representative of the actual family to "keep" this person with them to make him participate in criminal actions in the interest of Cosa Nostra with the exclusion of crimes of blood.

XXIII

It takes only one woman to make, in less than the time it takes to make a minestrone, a whole brood of children, offer your hand one day, stand in tie and tails, and suddenly you're in prison or a stupor, without so much as a piece of cheese. Put your head under water to banish the devils. You scratch your head, say you should have been one of the soldiers instead; suddenly the minestrone becomes a chamber pot and you're an old man who can never go out in the nasty weather.

CENT'ANNI FA: CINQUE FIGLI E 35 ANNI DI VITA MEDIA.
OGGI: UN FIGLIO E QUASI 80 ANNI.

XXIV

In Italia it is easier to find a fountain than a chamber pot. But if you go to the right party you have a chance to dance with the legs of Lily rather than quarrel with a wicked woman, which would later make you feel like an eel slithering into the garden. Even a hunter needs occasionally to take communion. Ask any bird; even a wicked woman is not content to be a piece of meat.

But today it makes an echo, except using a more modern language, that of psychoanalyst Luce Irigaray, theoretician of difference: "Only a sexual right, that keeps track of the diversity of women, will give them a true identity."

XXV

You can pray all you like to St. Anthony, until you're an old man, but you'll never be able to cut off the hunchback's hump with a knife. The palace guards beat him for praying to St. Anthony again to find that which regards only the ground: what hides under her skirt, but then I saw them kneeling themselves, with hands folded. Only a fool would throw a tomato at somebody's head as a cure for lice, but that's what he did, then he took that same knife to slice cheese. Finally he had a good cry. But honestly, would you rather inhabit an old house or a palace? Forget it, the way you dress, you'd never get past the guards.

These gestures have a weight before God, that the man, precisely because he sins, is truly a free person.

XXVI

It's a disgrace, those tits, says the old woman, if the baby cannot suck from them and you are not a mother, they merely encourage the drunk to remain in a stupor, consorting with devils. It's a disgrace to wear a tuxedo through nasty weather just to have a glass of wine.....

In this manner, inside the security acquired in this circular journey, the Italian woman seems to have finally both desire and capacity to look inward, to gather together in one long embrace mothers, grandmothers and great-grandmothers, to pay them the debt in her state of full consciousness.

XXVII

It's a disgrace to eat minestrone with your hand, I know that hand is the one with which you fondle the balls of the lieutenant, I've heard him call you his tomato, I know because I am your mother, even though you call me the hairy one, and no matter how many times I go to mass, Italy is nothing but a lifetime of miserable weather for me: I dream of a thief and a knife, and no hospital exists in which one can be cured of a murder already committed, no hospital exists for a murdered spirit, because the first flesh of my flesh is a drunk, and the second a word even death shouldn't speak.

There is a fantasy of family that precedes and accompanies the real family. There is an unconscious family, a "family of night" attached to the daytime family, that each one lives in reality; this unconscious family often enters into conflict with the real, to the point that, if we do not learn to recognize it, can create terrible conflicts.

XXVIII

The mouth of my bride is also the mouth of my mother, and that gives a man of honor fear, you go to a party searching for maidens and soon enough you're roasting chestnuts with devils, no longer a man of honor. What is the point of the 33 years of Christ, when a knife could just as easily be used on the cat or the rooster? Or those soldiers who seem to have taken root underneath the balcony of the woman who should but will never belong to me.

Women I have always understood afterwards—never or rarely at the right moment. I asked for sex and they wanted love, I passed on to love and they wanted passion, and if I completed the mistake in saying love and passion, yes, but also intellect, they were offended to death...

XXIX

The balls of the lieutenant are as much a piece of meat as the legs of Lily, just ask the hunchback. You won't see him in tie and tails at church on Christmas, or the old man or the fool. Wouldn't that be a disgrace? How many sins are already brought like flowers to church or waxed sacs of cheese roped across a horse, as if there had been a death in the palace?

Because in the Italian woman more than in others of diverse cultures—it seems to me—there is apparent an almost naïve movement between body and spirit. You search for the body and they are spirit, and you search for spirit and they are there, very bodily.

XXX

If I found the blood of an eel on my grave I would pray to the Virgin, then ask the monk to say mass as he did for me after the quarrel that prompted the guards to take me to prison where I remained until I was the man who speaks from death. Only in Italy I take off my hat when I pass the fountain to catch my ever- flowing tears.

In the heart of the boss there is also a place of pardon, provided the transgressions are venial sins: an inadvertent rudeness to another affiliate, an order not executed...And often on the occasion of Christmas or Easter, the commission concedes an amnesty.

XXXI

The lice in the hair of a man of honor would not be visible to the woman at the balcony, gazing down at his balding head, even if the man of honor, in tie and tails, had removed his hat in courtesy, and thrust toward her flowers, which might have had as their destination a mass or a party. But the baby, the cat, and the old woman closer to the ground, see also the eel he conceals beneath tie and tails. St. Guiseppe, however, is good enough to overlook.

Offer prosciutto and mozzarella and they would like flowers, succeed in executing that curious operation of entering the florist and then running errands with flowers in your hand, but then or later you realize it isn't over, they want presents too, in particular the ones celebrating birthdays and saint's days, and that if you don't give those, when it is YOUR turn they make huge presents to make clear how much greater is their affection.

XXXII

A father of children without a bride is like Italy without the tomato. Even the hunchback can find a woman eventually with the help of soldiers, if he dresses up as Pulcinella, if he gets only drunk on water from the fountain and buys bread only from the shopkeeper who helps the fountain's water turn to tears when he admits his fear.

But if you insist with flowers and presents they begin to think you are spending as little as possible on them, miser that you are, yes, it is clear you send flowers and presents in order not to sign checks. And they turn it over in their minds until one day it explodes: all the stories and history and explanations of your stinginess that as such has spoiled the presents and flowers that now don't count any more, and there is the need to begin all over again progressing from carnations to red roses, from pendants to necklaces to even bigger, gaudier gold....

XXXIII

Because of the devil, the fall: our sins; because of our sins, the 33 years of Christ, the death that speaks, and hence Christmas; at Christmas, communion to feed the spirit. But don't forget, inside the palace is a cannon; behind its walls an old man lures maidens with cheese, then takes them over his knee to spank. Spirit or no spirit, I'm no fool.

Note: This story is composed of thirty-three narratives derived from randomly ordered elements of the Italian game called TOMBOLA. Each alternate paragraph consists of "found" material from the Italian magazines Panorama and L'Espresso, which the author has taken the liberty of translating. Any mention of actual persons or places is used for fictional purposes only.

AN ETRUSCAN CATECHISM

The priest plows a straight line with the assistance of one white ox and one white cow, the furrow he makes acknowledged by all Etruscans as a sacred boundary. The city stands watching, reverent, attentive; the engineers stand ready to build and to tunnel. Then what sprouts up from the new-plowed earth? A flower? A rock? A colony of worms? No, a head; a baby's head, or rather face, grafted onto a white-haired head, is born from the earth, but attached to this head is a dwarf's stunted body. The body's hand thrusts something toward us: a book.

IT IS WRITTEN in The Book of Tages that the liver of the sacrificed sheep will be divided into four sections, which are each in turn divided into four, and these comprise the organ's outer edge only, within which still more divisions occur, repeating some of those found in the sixteen. The whole of the liver's houses' sum is forty-four, and each is affiliated with particular gods in the heavens.

WHO IS TAGES?

He is the source of Etruscan sacred law. He is unmistakable: a creature with the body of a dwarf, the smooth face of a child, and the head of an old man, who emerged from the soil like a beetle or worm to deliver our sacred knowledge.

WHAT IS THE NUMBER OF GODS IN THE HEAVENS?

The sum of our gods is sixteen

WHERE ARE THE GODS LOCATED ON THE LIVER?

In all three regions of the north eastern quadrant we find Tinia, whose head squeezed out his goddess daughter, Menvra, at birth, winged and in full armor, bearing a shield. The liver's seat, meanwhile, is occupied by Ani Thne and Mulciber. Cetha is in the eighth, while Letham in the 12 and 13th, comprises the Fates. In the sixteenth dwells Nocturnus, god of night. *After many years of tactile practice, the haruspex's fingers know one god from another, even without the assistance of his eyes.*

WHERE ARE THE SUN AND MOON LOCATED?

On the liver's underside which is divided into the two major divinities of sun and moon: Usils and Tivr.

HOW ARE THE BOLTS ASSIGNED TO THE VARIOUS GODS?

Nine gods are designated to hurl one or more of the eleven kinds of thunderbolts available. Tinia hurls three thunderbolts whereas Uni his wife hurls one.

WHEN DO THEY PERFORM THEIR ACTIVITY?

Menvra Cilens, guardian of the gates, hurls by night, and Sethlans and Mars participate as well. A trained haruspex does not have to make an equation but will know when the rumble or flash occurs, that this is the hand of Mars, or Tinia, that this bolt is Uni's sign. There will be no need to convert, it will be as quick as the flash itself, just as the calculation of a temple's length is automatic when its width is known, just as ejaculation of the gods is sure to send white shooting through the sky and cause the body of the mortal who receives it to tingle in a corresponding manner.

WHAT CAN THE GODS DO?

In addition to the hurling of thunderbolts and lightning, they are responsible for all fortune, good and ill, of mortals. They can also do injury to each other, as did Sethlans—to his mother Uni—imprisoning her in the throne he built, and from which later he released her. They can decorate the sky in a variety of ways: make it awash with light, as when sleeping Hera's breast was wrenched in astonishment from the lips of full-grown suckling Hercules, spawning the milky way, or they can sear it with a lightning bolt from any arbitrary quadrant.

WHAT CAN AN ETRUSCAN DO?

Many things, both remarkable and unremarkable. An Etruscan can build and plan and drain, change the course of rivers, irrigate, navigate, play and dance persuasively enough to drive away the plague, if for instance called upon by unsuccessful Roman neighbors, less renowned in arts of movement, creativity and divination—neighbors who might prove useful in Etruscan games when blood is required to appease the ghosts of our ancestors. This is required only on special occasions, however, whereas on any given day an Etruscan, male or female, is likely to wear a tebennos if a man, and a chiton only partially covering his body; a light-weight longer pleated tunic if a woman. Both are likely to step every morning into handsome red shoes high in back and pointy in front, or bronze thonged high-soled sandals. A man might have a beard or shave, perhaps wear a toque; a woman might braid or coil her hair, or have tight curls to frame her face, or plaited hair tucked into a cap. She would likely toast her husband and his friends, drink wine, write and read. But there is more than this to what Etruscans, male and female, do. He or she can import joy to every movement. He or she can make of any gesture music. He or she can even make a dance of defecation.

IS THERE ANYTHING AN ETRUSCAN CANNOT DO?

An Etruscan cannot avoid the will of the gods. He or she cannot see the dawn rise over the sea. In certain instances he cannot avoid the aggression of animals if the gods will his defeat or if he is distracted by more urgent sensations than his fear. For example, he cannot defeat a dog if the dog is at his heel and driven by another man, while his senses are impeded by a hood over his head. It is without question better to wear a head punctuated by a haruspex's pointy hat, aligned with heaven, than to wear a hat of humiliation, that shrouds the victim's face, and makes vulnerable the entire body underneath. Even more desirable would be to have the head of a god which sprouts another fully formed tiny god as hat, a hat which thus has limbs and wings and shield and even helmet.

But one might wish to have no head at all, when in the midst of being entered from behind, he suddenly finds himself nearly face to face with the horn of an oncoming bull. *In such instances irony might cause an Etruscan to smile, displaying the beautifully worked gold dentistry for which we are widely known.* For no other reason, in fact, than to bridge his teeth may an Etruscan import gold into his tomb. And most importantly of all, golden-mouthed or otherwise, an Etruscan cannot under any circumstances avoid abduction to the underworld by the fierce pair Charun and Telulcha. *Irony might cause an Etruscan to smile, when after importing her many bronze mirrors and cosmetic boxes, spatulae and jewels, and carefully plaiting her hair, her escort to the underworld is a harpy-haired creature whose hideous snakes snarl her braids, whose donkey ears and vulture face and blue skin are far more dramatic than any style she could concoct by means of the aforementioned accouterments.* If the hammer in Charun's hand suspended over her skull paralyzes her in fear, however, she is unlikely to smile, swiftly noting that the persuasiveness of his tool makes a mockery of any weapon bulging from the tomb's wall, articles all carefully fashioned for her comfort and protection, as she surrenders to an irony more literally striking.

WHAT CAN A HARUSPEX DO TO MEDIATE BETWEEN THE GODS AND MEN?

In general, observe, interpret and advise, and from these three come all the more specific gestures. He relies upon his hands and eyes, to read the signs that populate the sky and to interpret with his fingers imperfections on the liver's surface.

LET US REVIEW

By the height of his hat a haruspex connects us to heaven. By the breadth of his knowledge he answers our questions: reminds us the length and the width of our temple is equal; he records the location and number of birds in the sky at all times, the number of bolts thrown from heaven between dusk and dawn by the gods. Furthermore he distinguishes which god threw which bolt; furthermore he is never in error.

HOW DOES HE AVOID ERROR?

Would you mistake a cock for a turd, simply because one enters where the other exits, or because the posture of a man receiving the former and excreting the latter is in some cases similar? Would you mistake a dwarf for a haruspex, or a horse for a fish, or a whip for a flute, or the earth for the sea, simply because you inhabit land and water with equal pleasure? Surely you would not confuse West with East or you could never be a haruspex (for all Etruscans know that good fortune derives from the East, and all that derives from the West is unfavorable.) Can a bird be a fish? And yet there are times when a horse becomes fish: when each lends half its nature to a third hybrid creature. A man is, however, less likely to ride such a beast; his knees might lose their grip and his body slide off; instead of meeting the barrier of horse's haunches he'd find himself straddling a slippery tapering cylinder. That is our mascot: hippocampus. There are, however, far worse fates than to feel the horse between one's legs become fish, for an Etruscan is also intimate with water, and rides its waves as well as he rides land. It is preferable, for instance, to ride a hippocampus than to be a slave in disfavor, although even a slave in disfavor is not denied the lyre's consolations. One need not be a haruspex to know that in Etruruia no scourging occurs unaccompanied by double flute or lyre or castanets, though perhaps this is custom rather than law. And yet when the creature who emerges from the soil to give our sacred laws has an old man's head, a dwarf's body and the smooth unlined face of a child, we know a force of strangeness drives the world, a force we raise our arms and leap into the air to meet; we bend our bodies forward, even contort ourselves to greet the strangeness that compels us as our nature.

IS THE HARUSPEX EXCLUDED FROM THESE REVELS?

The haruspex is not excluded from our revels, but he cannot be a full participant in celebration, as we have designated him observer. His eye must miss nothing, and his hands must not be occupied with trifles, not with kneading or beating time for he must count the duration of thunderclaps, and his feet cannot either be captured by music, for they must be placed one at right angle to the other on the boulder that likely as not is a meteor sent us from heaven. Thus he must at all times offer full attention to his sacred tasks. He must observe all that pertains to his concerns, and of line—be it crooked or jagged or straight—he remains the undisputed legislator.

BUT TELL ME WHAT USE HAS THE HARUSPEX FOR THE CURVE OF A CAPE?

its red fabric draped over shoulder or hip, what use for the curve of a wrestler's firm thigh harmonized with the elegant shapely libation dish placed between himself and his opponent: two wrestlers who lock forearms as they struggle to declare the victor, gazing only at each other, and not at the birds overhead or the augur gesturing toward the birds as he interprets their flight, or the pair of less equally matched opponents to his right: one sighted one blinded, a dog in between, the latter clearly disadvantaged: one man at the mercy of man and beast.

Indeed, what would cause a haruspex to dwell on the convexity of the boxer's belly, a curve which to the Romans is displeasing, suspicious—like the curve of our slightly slanted eyes—but to us, Etruscans, sensuous, perhaps less relevant to the haruspex than the surprising convexity of an implement or artifact that protrudes from the wall, placed there by those we love, to give ballast as we approach the underworld.

IS IT THE TASK OF THE HARUSPEX TO FURNISH OR DECORATE THE TOMB? IS IT HE WHO CHOOSES ITS OCCUPANTS?

No, he only counsels, he does not choose the wreath or vase or parasol, those greaves or axe or helmet, rope or wooden tray, and he might echo our sentiments when we remark, how curious to find a wall tumescent instead of flat. For what is a wall if not a surface to lean against after too much dancing or too much wine, after the exertion of blowing into the mouth of the bronze trumpet or dispatching a rapid succession of exhalations into the double flute, or in the wake of a sensation of communion so overwhelming that it makes of two humans for moments a third hybrid creature, and whose aftermath of closure requires a surface to lean upon in order to reconstitute their separate selves.

HOW CURIOUS INDEED THAT THE UNFLAT WALL ERUPTS IN SHAPES

which do not mean to disconcert but to console, such as the shield to protect from the blows of Charun's hammer which is poised to deliver the blow that abducts her to the underworld, against which there is very little even the haruspex can do to intervene, as it was not he, in the first place, if what you say is true, who deposited her there.

This is exactly so. For all his powers of concentration, all his knowledge and training, he cannot change the will of Herc or Menvra, Fulfuns, Uni; the gods will what the gods will, and the role of the haruspex is not to intercede but to advise. "Abase yourself to Silens who sent this bolt," he might suggest, or "Beg mercy from Sethlans who is displeased with you, perhaps because of where you stood a certain time of day, and do not forget that lightning could strike twice from different sectors, for some gods, like Tinia, occupy more than one house."

BUT WAS THAT NOT HE WHO SEATED THE COUPLE AT THE TABLE?

Or reclined them on their brocaded banquet couch; was that not the curve of her body in his arms, drapery of her tunic flowing, as he set her on the sarcophagus, was he not placing her upon the hard bed, laying her head gently on the stone pillow? I heard he even set the banquet table, fastening the miniature cluster of grapes made of bronze at her earlobe, and braided her hair, and placed a book in her hand for her journey.

You are mistaken, for all the while he stands with left foot on boulder, left hand on left knee, right foot at right angle while right hand reads the dark eviscerated meat. The only ornament he touches is the fibula he fastens at his neck. The only fabric draping is his own pleated tunic; he never fingered the soft fleshy part of her lower ear, he holds only the lobes of the liver draped over his palm.

YOU ARE SO CERTAIN OF THE HARUSPEX'S ACTIONS.
TELL ME THEN AND BY WHAT METHODS EXACTLY, AS
HE HOLDS THE LOBES, MIGHT HE AVOID ERROR?

It is a matter of comparison, when over and over a sheep submits to slaughter, such that liver begets liver and organ after organ is compared with the memory of another, prior, repository of signs, which in contrast to what the uninitiated might suspect, do not blend, and become one, but rather gain distinction in their sequence; each astoundingly unique. Thus while other citizens before dawn dream in bed or linger at the banquet table, noting only casually, for beauty's sake, the moon and stars' illumination, cast upon the delicate divergences of flesh rotating wife to servant, husband, lover, toasting each other with bucchero cups and libation dishes, consuming grains and olives, fish and game, then still sated, arranging themselves on their couches or retiring to their private chambers drinking from more secret vessels, thinking in their lovers' hubris, in one organ I can read the universe; even more so can the haruspex who, elsewhere stands, solitary, angled in dawn's nascent light to touch again and again that extracted organ divided meticulously into houses though removed from its own house.

BUT WHAT THEN IS A BODY? A WHOLE DIVIDED INTO
PARTS?

A body is, in part, the breast or testicle the festive lover weighs in a hand and exclaims over, boasting, to the other banqueting guests, although it can also be that of her which is hidden under a costume's folds when dancing, that of him more likely visible, or the part of Hera which the mouth of Hercules sought even full grown (and which ejaculated milk into the sky as statement of surprise) or the four burgeoning pendulous udders of the leopard who has borrowed the teats of the cow.

In certain instances a body is comprised of both twinned parts of the creature that supports itself erect in front with legs and swims behind, galloping and flapping in a single gesture.

IF A BODY IS DIVIDED INTO PARTS THEN CAN A SINGLE PART ITSELF DIVIDE?

Yes, for instance, a head can be both that which sprouts snakes from a vulture's face and droops a donkey's ears, in the case of the creature who is half of the pair that escorts an unfortunate Etruscan to the underworld: a creature who proliferates parts, for he wears many beasts as a head: a head that perhaps might continue to undulate while his body reposed, were he ever to sleep, and give our people respite from intimidation.

Alternatively, one part can flower into a secondary whole, as in the story of the god who excreted a goddess from his head in birth. Whereas usually we find wedged between the head and feet a trunk; in this case head supports another's feet and not the feet one's own head.

More disquieting still is a situation in which a man finds himself in the center of a collision from both ends as he faces a charging bull, when that part of another man behind him which visits his rear is divided itself into body and head; is a rod with a hat and its hat called head, so that man in the middle serves as a wedge between horned head of beast and headed horn of a man, the latter which in effect fastens for moments a tail to the man's tail (as the two men fleetingly craft of themselves a third hybrid creature that is, alas, even in its ingenuity hardly a match for the bull.) Thus all of the man between tail and head comprises a wedge between two forces, one brutal, one benign.

BUT COULD IT NOT BE THAT THE HUMAN PLEASURE IS ATTRIBUTABLE ONLY TO THE SECOND MAN?

And that he in fact forces that pleasure on the first man, and that perhaps the bull, sensing the victim's distress, approaches to lick his face and not to ravage? Perhaps he will leap over him to assault the man behind him? Furthermore, what of the considerably paler third creature, faintly visible, whose back is supported by the back of the kneeling man. Is it woman, man, or beast?

I can see nothing you describe, although it compels. But allow me to finish. Most curiously, and disturbingly of all, a head can be more than divided, erased: when it is that part of an Etruscan which is hardly visible because it is covered with a hood, as in the case of a participant in funeral games: a man pursued by a dog who tugs at the leash held by a second man who follows close behind and seems to make no effort to restrain the creature whose teeth sear the flesh of the barefoot man's calf—the second man seeming in fact to use the leash of the dog to restrain not the dog but the man, who cannot—despite the all but useless cudgel in his hand, entangled, as it is, like ankle, shoulder, wrist in a red rope that flowers in the collar around the dog's neck,—arrest this abuse, retaliate or defend himself, in part because his senses are impeded by the hood which he, not by his own choice surely, has covered his head, and which like ankle, shoulder and wrist, is ensnared by the binding red line.

CAN A DOUBLE FLUTE WALK?

Two cylinders poked with holes? More easily than can this man after his arduous participation in the game the gods chose for him to play and we sought fit to set to music.

AND WHAT OF THE HARUSPEX WHO PLUCKS FROM ONE WHOLE ONE PART, ONLY FURTHER TO DIVIDE HIS PRIZE, OSTENSIBLY TO REPRESENT A GREATER WHOLE? WHAT IS HIS RELATION TO THESE PARTS?

Obviously a haruspex would have less desire to ride the exuberant curve of a dolphin's sleek back as it decorates the sea, than to attend to the arc of the bird that the augur, hand to forehead in a gesture of mourning, watches, beside the doors to the underworld. What use for the arc of the stone that is hurled from the boy's slingshot, as he stands poised with bent knee behind him and the toe of the forward leg curling over a precipice, without fear or awkwardness, at the bird about to be eliminated from the flock which soars above him, and may in its diminution bode ill for his future, but only the haruspex can discern, not the boy, surely not the boy, as he stands joyfully oblivious on a precipice above the boat over whose hull leans another boy who dangles his red, precisely measured line, held slack between two hands, pinched at each termination between thumb and forefinger, lowered into the green of the sea's banquet, while from another precipice plunges the diver's body, head first, about to penetrate the wet surface adjacent to the site of the boy's line as his feet uphold the sky. He does not question if the water will receive him; he assumes his welcome, like a fish.

WHAT SIGNIFICANCE IS ASCRIBED TO THE HEIGHT OF A HAT, THE LENGTH OF A COCK, THE NUMBER OF BIRDS OR OF BOLTS IN THE SKY?

The duration of rumbling over our heads that our feet feel, our ears hear but that cannot be seen? The length and the width of the temple, the depth of the tomb—itself a product of skilled engineering—the distance from object to object affixed to the wall of the tomb, the depth of the diver's plunge into the sea, the distance the stone in the boy's slingshot travels, the size of the dancing man's turd, the duration of and distance between each pitch when the subolo places his mouth on the hole and sends breath through to please us, to balance the sound of the whip's repetition, the cries of the woman or man being beaten, the moans of the boar and the deer as the net ensnares?

Your questions, your questions, I am suddenly weary of so many questions!

WHAT IS THE SIGNIFICANCE OF THE NUMBER OF PRISONERS TAKEN IN BATTLE?

And only later slaughtered as offering to appease the ancestors, and thus indirectly the gods, in the hope that less lightning derive from the west, that the shed blood of Romans will mitigate wrath and elicit their favor, that the shed blood of Romans will serve as deterrent, as surrogate, sparing Etruscan blood?

I do know that no activity, be it brutal or benign, should lack the sweetness of music. Music can act as the smooth unlined face of a child to sweeten a stunted withered body; music can make a whole of a half-horse half-fish.

AND WHAT IS THE RELATION OF THE HARUSPEX TO MUSIC?

While all around him move in a continuum of revelry and cele-bration, performing ordinary daily gestures, in attitudes of reverence, love, or recklessness, brutality and viciousness, exalted or quotidian, he is stationary; he does not beat with sticks or flutter fingers click-ing castanets, or thrum a lyre. Nor does he bake or knead or stir or drop a line into the sea. He does not hurl a stone at bird or fish or beat with club or wrestle an opponent. Neither does he sip from a libation dish at banquet table; he is unlikely to enfold a man or woman in his bed, and does not dance unless the subtle movements of his fingers are a dance.

WHAT ARE THE QUESTIONS MOST OFTEN ASKED OF THE HARUSPEX, AND WHAT IS THEIR TONE?

Desperate or importunate, most likely. For example: "What shall I place in my tomb to accompany me to the life below, and to whom shall I make a votive offering so as to right the consequences of the thunder's damage, and what tune shall I bid the subulo play as I scourge the servant for his misdeeds, and where shall we place the sacred furrow to declare the boundaries of the city?..."

THESE ARE RELENTLESS. ARE THERE NO SOFTER VOICES FOR THE HARUSPEX TO HEAR?

At times, he might hear voices such as this: O haruspex, I seek your counsel: tell me, if you hear, what sector of which god's will has led me to this place? What is its name? All is familiar yet I feel unmoored, unsure. Shall I have my parasol in my tomb? My comb, how many mirrors, haruspex? My lovely boxes of cosmetics in the shape of beasts? My earrings? Bracelets? Diadem? Will it ever again be warm enough to warrant my unfolding the fan folded into this wall of my tomb, my tomb, like some vertical table which houses famil-iar objects that comfort. Am I one among the dead then? When will life turned to death turn again? Will it turn to the Styx and return me from that brackish mirror to gaze in the one whose polished surface will offer a woman some centuries older, whose hair worn in ringlets, is now worn in braids, whose hair is coiled round, whose myths etched in bronze on the backs of these mirrors have entertained her for all the hours she spent of her lives braiding or coiling or curling, adorning neck and wrists, fastening jewelry and painting her face more often than not for the man who once done with the nubile obliging servants would find her again in the bed, interrupting her reading, to read all the lines of her flesh. And she said to him often, I confess to you now, "your hands are so knowing, so gentle, if I loved the Etruscans, my people, more than my own pleasure I would insist you enter the vocation of the haruspex, caressing the liver of sheep after sheep as intently, as tenderly, sensuously, as you caress me."

LET US REVIEW

Again and again you plunge your hand into the interior cavity. Dawn and again you enter, another dawn and you enter to find yet another answer to a question not yet formulated; forage with your practiced hand in a warmth that still remembers life though life has left it, a life whose bleating you recall beseeching you, you who cannot spare one or another creature when the gods require you read a larger picture quietly encoded on the surface of this particular liver that once ruled its body now a larger measure: index of the universe. A sheep cannot expel the liver without the stewardship of your practiced hand, and thus you enter to inseminate and exit immediately with an afterbirth that is, in effect, your only child.

WHAT RESPONSES IS A HARUSPEX LIKELY TO GIVE TO THOSE ETRUSCANS WHO ARE BESET BY MISFORTUNE?

He must be sober but not lugubrious, for one can always abase oneself and hope for better in the future. It is necessary to remind the aggrieved who seek his counsel that all heaven's light cannot be from the East, and neither will all be from the West; misfortune will befall some citizens as surely as the dice will eventually display each of its faces: each of the letters that spell out our numbers, and for each misfortune and each fortune there is origin and we must honor all signs

that come from the gods; we must not favor only those which favor us, for that would comprise only half a cosmos.
IS THE ACCRETION OF MISFORTUNES BURDENSOME TO THE HARUSPEX? FOR EXAMPLE, DOES HE NEVER WISH IF TIME ALLOWED HIM TO INDULGE IN PLAY AS OTHER CITIZENS, PERHAPS TO RECOMMEND TO THEM THESE DISTRACTIONS IN CONJUNCTION WITH THEIR OFFERINGS TO THE GODS?

What possible use to the haruspex, who performs specialized tasks of gravity, to follow the curve of the discus thrown by a young man who eventually with great skill will extinguish the candle's flame in this manner, competing with his friends who take their turns to accomplish the questionable objective until the room is dark, altogether dark, with no bright tongue flickering to draw the eye; this is indeed an idle game and he would not disparage it, but he would have time neither to participate nor observe the haphazard curve in the earth made by the violent wheels steered by the charioteer, who if he is a young reckless man wraps the reins about his waist, causing them to encircle his form rather than be pulled taut and straight, thus creating a crease in the earth chaotic in comparison to the sacred furrow of the haruspex with his one white bull, one white cow as he sits somber under his tall hat driving a straight path almost all the way to the gates, clods turning inward always toward the city, knowing that Tages once greeted our people through just such earth to give the laws that dictate the very line he now creates. Clearly a man who drives the sacred plow does not perform ostentatious feats for entertainment or for competition; his concern is rather that unswerving line carefully etched into soil and terminated just short of the gates, so as to allow the unclean gods entrance and exit, for in this manner are the boundaries designed, and the city consecrated.

DOES THE HARUSPEX SEE ALL THINGS?

A haruspex, though mediator to them, is neither god nor godlike in his perspicacity, focused on the signs before his eyes; all that is peripheral is useless to him: the crowds gathered to celebrate the city's consecration do not divert his gaze from the furrow. For instance, he

would not once squint into the distance beyond these newly desig-
nated city limits, to take notice of the horizontal horn of a man's lower
body as it enters from the West the furrow of the curved buttocks
of the man who, bent before him, faces the horn of a beast from the
East, an oncoming bull who was never yoked to the plow of the
haruspex; in any case, it is as if the pleasure of what enters from
behind could save the man from what confronts him face to face per-
haps to rend his chest—although in another situation the beast
might just as easily turn away disinterested in the spectacle before him
when he reaches the man, now on his knees before his thrusting
partner, who on first glance thrusts in air, but upon closer scrutiny
enters a very pale figure barely visible, whose back is supported by the
kneeling man. In any case, and in all, it is for the gods to dictate.

WHY WOULD THIS MAN NOT ATTEMPT TO FLEE?

He will not likely flee, the man, for we are a people who roll the
dice even as famine demands more sober measures, even as the thun-
der in our bellies competes with the sky, for we know that pleasure
must never concede to danger or hardship. We play before plan-
ning, leap in lamenting, we'd rather dance to drive away the plague
than mourn. This is our solution, our equation, just as length and width
of temple is a given, so this measure offers balance. And while there
is perhaps no respite for the middle man, he would nonetheless pre-
fer to remain as he is, bent and yielding, vulnerable and aroused, to
keep his position intact rather than exchange his fate for the fate of
the man with shrouded head who has pleasure neither from creature
nor human. Even the feeble reed the buggered man clutches is more
solid than the cudgel held by the hooded man, entangled in the long
red line that, while it blossoms in the canine collar, baits him, with-
out mercy, like a fish.

AND WHAT OF YET ANOTHER MAN ON THE OTHER
SIDE SIMILARLY POSTURED, BENT FORWARD BUTTOCKS
JUTTING, HIS FOOT RAISED AS IF TO INITIATE SOME
RHYTHMIC SEQUENCE? IS HIS ACTIVITY OF CONCERN
TO THE HARUSPEX?

Continue to observe that man and you will see he merely augments the soil by offering to earth his plosive turd (as the brass trumpet somewhere sounds) not to be confused with the clods of soil turned always inward, lifted and moved if they fall outside the city's boundaries. However, if the haruspex, as he turned all the clods of soil in toward the city, discovered the careless man's turd, you can be sure his finger would find later, on the next liver over which he lingered, a mark indicting him.

CAN FATE TRULY BE DETERMINED THROUGH THESE SUBTLE INDICATORS?

Yes, from a mark on the liver or streak in the sky, swiftly etched and then just as swiftly retracted by the gods, never fixed in the manner of an image etched on a mirror's bronze back or letters scratched in papyrus: written, rather, in air; all the signs written in air on a tablet so dark and soft it has no edge, with a shape neither round nor square, a texture between solid and liquid, a substance consisting entirely of contour.

THEN IT TRULY IS OF CONSEQUENCE WHICH PART OF SKY THE BIRDS INSCRIBE AT DUSK, AT DAWN?

This question you can answer for yourself by now. We must conclude. I must be about my business.

I WILL ASK NO MORE IF YOU WILL TELL ME WHAT IS THE MOST TERRIBLE SECRET HARBORED BY THE HARUSPEX?

If you must be sated, I will answer. When the lightning tells him more than we might wish to know and when the birds squawk even at night and when the liver seems too densely inscribed with signs then who is he, he wonders, mere haruspex, to tell them that the very gold that crowns her teeth will one day, after Etruscans are no longer, be extracted like a liver from a sheep and all the carefully selected items plundered, subtracted one by one; the sweet, diverting stories borrowed from the Greek etched on the back of her bronze mirrors silenced as they melt back down to metal, their lump sum of origin; in the same manner that a trumpet's blustering wind might obliterate the ephemeral intoning of the lyre's strings, these stories will succumb to the bold raw lettering that spells SUTHINA on the polished surface. For is it not an indivisible sum and the most reliable of measures, that we who are expert at navigation and manipulation of all waters, at tunneling, sewage and hydraulics, cannot for all our mastery, divert the course of the River Styx?

Every shoot and every fruit is produced above the insertion (in the axil) of its leaf which serves as its mother, giving it water from the rain and moisture from the dew which falls at night from above, and often it protects them against the too great heat of the rays of the sun.
Leonardo Da Vinci

Set yourself to describe the beginning of man when he is created in the womb. And why an infant of eight months does not live.

Interventional treatment of the fetus before birth has been applied in such life-threatening conditions as hydrocephalus (fluid buildup in the brain) and hydroephrosis (a blockage of the urinary tract). The computer-enhanced image illustrates injection that passes through abdomen, uterus, and into fetal bladder.

What sneezing is.
What yawning is.

A picture made with ultrasound in the sixth month of pregnancy shows the face of a healthy fetus with mouth open in a yawn. "By this point the fetus does just about everything it will do after birth," said Dr. Christopher Merritt of New Orleans, who obtained the image. "It yawns, blinks, and even sucks its thumb."

In the year 1473, Leonardo assists his master Verrocchio with the painting, "The Baptism of Christ", in which two angels kneel together beside a standing, praying figure whose feet and ankles are submerged in water. The angel on the left, painted with astounding delicacy and fineness, by the apprentice, far surpasses the angel on the right, by the master. This moment is said by many in

Verrocchio's and other Florentine studios to be the beginning of Leonardo's painting career.

Probing painlessly, sonography uses sound waves to look within.

It is also the moment, in a sense, of my birth, although my actual birth was a decade later, for the angel painted by my master, Leonardo, bears an uncanny resemblance to my perpetually youthful self, whom he would discover on the streets of Milan at age ten, twenty years after executing that depiction, and rescue from poverty by taking into his home and training as servant, pupil, protégé, whatever term you choose. Labels matter little. My given Christian name, for example, is Giacomo, but you will know me by another name, with which my master re-christened me. Frankly, though—I'm accused of lying all the time ma sta volta sono sincero—I don't give a shit about painting. It makes me yawn.

In trouble before birth, Joseph Ward was found to have a tumor growing in his throat that forced him to keep his mouth open inside the womb.

SOMEWHERE, IN WHAT HAD BEEN UP UNTIL THEN A NEAR PERFECTLY HARMONIOUS COMMUNITY OF SOME ONE HUNDRED TRILLION CELLS, A NORMAL CELL BECOMES A CANCER CELL.

Trembling.
Epilepsy.
Madness.
Sleep.
Hunger.

My master eats no meat, and I, today, eat only candy: some aniseed sweets I was craving, and who would be so cruel as to take candy from a little boy? (A boy, moreover, with the appearance of an angel.) Alright, I admit that I stole the money he had put aside to make my jerkins with. Have you never had a craving?

Sensuality

To spy on the brain in action, PET scanners watch the way brain cells consume substances such as sugar. The substance is tagged with a radioisotope brewed in a small, low-energy cyclotron.

His name for me, Salai, means limb of Satan. As to which, the name or my behavior, is chicken and which is egg, I cannot say. I leave to you.

...stating which part of it is formed first, and so successively putting in its parts according to the periods of pregnancy until birth and how it is nourished, learning partly from the eggs laid by hens.

He says I break his heart when I make mischief. But he has never thrown me out or threatened to.

The heart of itself is not the beginning of life but is a vessel made of dense muscle vivified and nourished by an artery and a vein as are the other muscles.

The heart of the system is a piezoelectric crystal that converts electric pulses into vibrations that can penetrate the body. The sound waves are reflected back to the crystal, which reconverts them into electric signals. Echoes from the fetus are translated into faint signals, which are processed by the computer into a video image.

When women say that the child is sometimes heard to cry within the womb, this is more likely to be the sound of wind which rushes out...

What about your mother, master? Who sang to you and gave you milk?

To generate a US image a transducer in the shape of a small rod-like microphone is placed in contact with the surface of the body. A signal of high frequency in the range of 2 to 10 MHz (millions of cycles per second) is transmitted through the skin....The time delay between sending the pulse and receiving the reflection determines the depth of the target.

Why the thunderbolt kills a man and does not wound him, and if the man blew his nose he would not die.

How many profiles can you list? My master has a handsome collection of noses, but not all of them handsome. Are you in a bulbous mood today? Lunedì, aquiline; martedì, straight; mercoledì, pointed; giovedì, concave; venerdì, snub; sabato, round; domenica, regular. Shall we review? Take a deep breath and then take up your pencil.

It is impossible to breathe through the nose and through the mouth at the same time. The proof of this is seen when anyone breathes with the mouth open taking the air in through the mouth and sending it out through the nose, for then one always hears the sound of the gate set near to the uvula when it opens and shuts.

A padded compression plate is lowered from above and gently squeezes the breast to facilitate better imaging of the entire breast. The patient is told to hold her breath as views are taken of each breast.

Because it hurts the lungs.

The radiologist in this case is looking for a pulmonary embolism (a clot in the lung's blood supply.) Ten percent of cases of pulmonary embolism are fatal, so quick detection and therapy are usually of urgent concern.

My master hops from patron to patron to keep us fed. But every time one of them dies, he takes an interest in that particular disease and seeks to understand its workings, thus adding new distractions to his painting projects. If he were quicker with his work, this wouldn't be a problem. Perhaps they died of waiting, I say, surely there's a cure for that: just make art, Leonardo!

The classic form of Kaposi's sarcoma is rare and tends to strike men of Italian, Mediterranean and Eastern European Jewish heritage from their 50's to their 80's. It also occurs as an endemic form in African men.

Figure to show from whence comes the semen.
Whence the urine.
Whence the milk.

Lurking deep within the lobes and ducts of the breast, abnormal cells are detected by mammographic screening. In the color enhanced image to the left (side view of a breast) the small black dot surrounded by a contour of colors indicates a malignancy.

"I fed you with milk like my own son," you complain, in a voice that deserves the accompaniment of your infamous lira da braccio, ready to break into sobbing. You make it sound as if I sucked it straight from your tit. Let's get it straight; are you my mother or my master?

Whence come tears.
Whence the turning of the eyes when one draws the other after it.
Of sobbing.

Stop bawling! Send me home. Go find a wife; go have your own son.

To get a first hand idea of just how difficult (but very rewarding) the film interpretation process can be, I traveled to Rochester, New York to spend a day with Dr. Wende W. Logan, one of the busiest mammographers in the country. Her patients call her "Eagle Eye" for her ability to see things that others cannot.

The light, or pupil of the human eye, on its expansion and contraction, increases and decreases by half its size. In nocturnal animals it increases and decreases more than a hundred fold in size. This may be seen in the eye of an owl, a nocturnal bird, by bringing a lighted torch near its eye, and more so if you make it look at the sun.

From the back of a great swan, my master says, a man shall someday fly, and so he builds and treats and smears and plans: with pine upon lime, feather on canvas, sized silk; fashioning platforms and rudders and cables and windmills and undercarriages and something that looks like a giant shoe, the last of which is of least use to me, as I cannot steal it to sell to the shoemaker for aniseed sweets. What will be

next? eMadonna! It's another original contraption by Da Vinci, get
out of the way; stai attento! Before it crashes against the palace wall!

Then you will observe the pupil which previously occupied the
whole eye, diminished to the size of a grain of millet.

The smooth patches of skin that characterize Kaposi's are described by doc-
tors as nodules, plaques and macules; they vary in size from that of peas to that
of large coins.

There are many kinds of breast cancers, Dr. Logan told me. Some are as
small as fine grains of sand that "pepper" an area of the breast.

With this reduction it compares to the pupil of man, and the
clarity and brightness of objects appear to it of the same intensity since at this time they appear to man in the same proportion
because the brain of this animal is smaller than the brain of man.

The planning of 3-D treatment uses new techniques such as the "Beam's Eye
View." It is as if the human eye were placed at the exact position of the ori-
gin of the radiation and watched where it went.

Sight is better at a distance than near at hand with men who are
somewhat advanced in years because the same thing transmits
a smaller impression of itself to the eye when it is remote than
when it is near.

What do you want from a street urchin? You always seem surprised
that vulgar things should issue from these cherub lips? But you don't
know the viler things the eMilanese say. (All eyebrows raise imme-
diately, of course.) Everyone knows I'll never make a painting on my
own, that these wasted hours of instruction only allow you to gaze in
my angelic eyes. But in the master one cannot excuse incompetence.
It doesn't take much talent, Uncle Leonardo, it doesn't take a second
sight or even a trained eye to see that the painting you've been work-
ing on for years still isn't finished yet. Just like the one before it,
and.....shall we name names, and dates?

All things seen will appear larger at midnight than at midday and larger in the morning than at midday.

Shall we begin with March 16th, 1478 at St. Bernard's Chapel: the absent altar painting, which despite the receipt of 25 florins (and some persuasion on your father the notary's part) you never created—this first adult commission a striking contrast to your first work as a child, when your alacrity sustained the stench of decomposing animals in your room as you assembled a dragon's face so fierce your father sent you straight away to study with Verrochio, ostensibly to mine your talent subito—-but I think otherwise: your father was afraid of keeping such bizarre imagination in his own house, alive inside his little bastard, what's more! In any case, the Madonna, in maturity, did not sustain your inspiration in the same way. Admit it, you prefer a dragon to a virgin!

The wrinkles or folds of the vulva have indicated to us the position of the gate-keeper of the castle, which is always found where the meeting of the longitudinal wrinkles occurs. However, this rule is not observed in the case of all these wrinkles but only in those which are large at one end and narrow at the other, that is, pyramidal in shape.

The opening of brothels is no deterrent, is it, for the Florentine perversion known in certain studios, so prevalent in fact it needs no mention. And yet there is sufficient interest from my master to design a brothel so discreet that clients have at their disposal secret staircases to exit, enter. Artisans might climb such stairs, if only with intent to draw, observe, and draw still more into the night. Perhaps he'll slip himself between the putta and her client, then whip out his pen: "Per piacere, madonna, open, if you would, your thighs; my study lacks a female organ and I must, if only in duty to nature, be thorough.

THE EPIDEMIOLOGY OF CERVICAL CANCER IS EXTENSIVELY DOCUMENTED (THE WALTON REPORT 1982). INCREASED INCIDENCE IS ASSOCIATED WITH EARLY INTERCOURSE, MULTIPLE SEX PARTNERS, EARLY PREGNANCY, LARGE FAMILIES, LOW SOCIOECONOMIC STATUS, AND POOR PERSONAL HYGIENE. IT IS RARE IN NUNS AND JEWISH

WOMEN....THREE TYPES OF VIRUSES ARE COMMONLY ASSOCIATED WITH CERVICAL CANCER: HERPES SIMPLEX TYPE 2 (HSV2), CYTOMEGALOVIRUS, AND PAPILLOMA VIRUSES.

But how peculiar it looks, master: this souvenir you sketched: like an unadorned aperture: a lipless mouth, no fleshy rim to feel the sensation of a kite's tail tapping, tapping, gently tapping. More like the mouth of a cave.

The woman commonly has a desire quite the opposite of that of man. This is, that the woman likes the size of the genital member of the man to be as large as possible, and the man desires the opposite in the genital member of the woman, so that neither one nor the other ever attains his interest because Nature, who cannot be blamed, has so provided because of parturition. Woman has in proportion to her belly a larger genital member than any other species of animal.

It has occurred to me at last, master, the formula for finishing that you lack. There is no mare, no donna to dispel fatigue, and thus few paintings ever proceed beyond the inevitable impasse at which you weary yet again of the brush.

For I once saw a mule which was almost unable to move due to the fatigue of a long journey under a heavy burden, and which, on seeing a mare, suddenly its penis and all its muscles became so turgid that it multiplied its forces and to acquire such speed that it overtook the course of the mare which fled before it and which was obliged to obey the desires of the mule.

A standalone, dedicated machine (a 'mule') may be assigned the task of testing all new software coming into the firm. The security measures applied to the mule must be impeccable because the consequences of an undetected infection on this machine will be severe: all incoming software will be infected. Physical security is also essential: access should be limited to the mule's operator, and the machine should be locked when not in use.

Obviously you have no time to cultivate these conventional appetites and perceptions. Already you must make up for lost time. Into every Milanese ear it has been whispered that the coating you put on the wall of the Santa Maria della Grazie is as water to the walnut oil with which Christ and the apostles are painted; thus they are destined to fade and peel. They are already disappearing. You might have spared yourself the effort of The Last Supper. There will be no feast on the table for posterity, Leonardo.

Thus the liver becomes desiccated and like congealed bran both in color and in substance, so that when it is subjected to the slightest friction, its substance falls away in small particles like sawdust and leaves behind the veins and arteries.

The positrons collide with the electrons, and the two annihilate one another, releasing a burst of energy in the form of gamma rays. These rays shoot in opposite directions and strike crystals in a ring of detectors around the patient's head, causing the crystals to light up.

As ever, against convention, you allowed Judas a halo—after procrastinating over a year before arriving at his proper face, while receiving 2000 ducats as annual salary (non c'è male)— because such distinctions were too crude for an artist of your sophistication, preferring to mark the traitor by posture and expression. I, however, if you like, could piss the nimbus round the traitor's head to make it apparent to the philistines who can't discern these subtleties. I'm just trying to make myself useful, as you've taught me.

That sound which remains or seems to remain in the bell after it has received the stroke is not in the bell itself but in the ear of the listener, and the ear retains within itself the image of the stroke of the bell which it has heard, and only loses it by slow degrees, like that which the impression of the sun creates in the eye, which only by slow degrees becomes lost and is no longer seen.

FOR A LONG TIME, MAYBE TWENTY OR THIRTY YEARS, THE CANCER CELL DIVIDES AGAIN AND AGAIN. EVEN WHEN THE DESCENDANTS NUMBER

IN THE BILLIONS, THE BODY EXHIBITS NO READILY APPARENT SIGN
OR SYMPTOM OF WHAT HAS BY THEN BECOME A SEMI-INDEPENDENT
MASS WITH ITS OWN BLOOD SUPPLY.

*I suppose you acquired your taste for preposterous projects from the
first of Verrochio's you witnessed: the gilded ball and cross atop the
bell tower of Santa Maria del Fiore in Firenze, long before my birth.
Giotto, who had made the bell tower itself, you wrote, was not content merely to emulate his master. Nor are you, Leonardo, except in
taking on ridiculous ambitions, which you, moreover, often can't
bring to fruition. (As for me, I have better things to do than emulate you. But here's a secret your Salai will never whisper in your ear:
he wishes he could steal some of your perseverance. I am ashamed that
nothing seizes my attention, except demanding your attention, any
way I can.)*

*The Doppler effect was first explained by the Austrian physicist Christian
Johann Doppler in 1842, and refers to the change in the frequency of sound
as an object moves in distance and velocity from a given point. If you are trans-
mitting sound waves through a blood vessel, the way the sound is returned
can signify subtle changes in blood flow.*

If a man jumps on the points of his feet
his weight does not make any sound.

*Dr. Kaposi reported that, until death occurred, the most persistent symptom
for which his patients required treatment was "the feeling of tension and pain
in the hands and feet."*

*I'll jump up and down and stamp my feet until you tell me who that
woman in our house is, with a name I've never heard before. The new
housekeeper is all you'll say. Where did she come from though? From
Vinci? Boys I am accustomed to in your house but a woman, this is
something new. Is she your mother, this Caterina? The mother of my
bastard master? I'll shake the house, I'll hold my breath until my face
turns blue! Chi è la donna nuova?*

Write why the campanile shakes at the sound of its bells.
Where flame cannot live no animal that draws breath can live.

In this case, a radioactive gas makes a picture after the first breath; more pictures are obtained after several minutes of inhaling and after the gas mixture has been exhaled and the patient is breathing room air. (Embolism, pneumonia, asthma, bronchitis, emphysema, and even cancer can be diagnosed by perfusion and ventilation scans. Radiation here is again at a very low level.)

I say that the blue which is seen in the atmosphere is not its own colour, but is caused by the heated moisture having evaporated into the most minute imperceptible particles, which the beams of the solar rays attract and cause to seem luminous against the deep intense darkness of the region of fire that forms a covering above them.

Researchers say severe childhood sunburns and teenage sunburns are more than twice as likely to lead to skin cancer.

The new image is displayed on a TV monitor and each density is assigned a color. As an example, pure black can be changed to blue, pure white can be displayed as bright orange. Other colors can fill in the intermediate densities; assignments of color can be arbitrary or standardized.

I say that the pink my master wears is silly, and I say he's a sissy, but if he wants to dress me up in green velvet ribbons and silver cloth and parade me all around ᘓMilano with him, why should I object? ᘓWhy not be pretty as a picture for the painter?

Every element of a virtual world is a design decision. What colors, shapes, and sounds should you use? What effects will your choices have on the user? How do you make something appear realistic, and does that really serve your purposes? How do you structure an application when you can make it do anything you want? How do you guide users when they can do anything they want—or anything might happen?

How the first picture was nothing but a line which surrounded the shadow of a man made by the sun upon a wall.

ALTHOUGH IT IS LIKELY THAT BREAST CANCER HAS BEEN AROUND SINCE MAN FIRST SCRATCHED ON THE WALL OF HIS CAVE, THE REAL THRUST OF ORGANIZED RESEARCH IN THIS COUNTRY BEGAN ONLY IN 1970.

Man has progressed from cave painting to canvas to camera and now to machine vision.

I am sick of your lines, figures, your studies, your instructions; Io, Giacomo, Io, Salai, sono stuffo! Sick of your bodies, your elegant insufferable doodles, dappertutto, pagina dopo pagina, your limbs and bones and lines, your wombs and vessels. Mi viene da vomitare. Capisci? I want to puke! And you do not deserve to know, but I am jealous of your grotesque faces, grim cadavers, for I believe at times they fascinate you more than I do, than my bland beauty. It is obscene to be so drawn to beauty as my master is, in all and in its most peculiar forms. Bellezza is his mistress; I am merely his inadequate apprentice. I want to leave this place, this post I never asked for, and crawl into a cave.

I WAS CURIOUS ABOUT THE OMISSION OF BREAST CANCER FROM THE CAVE AND WALL SCRATCHING OF PRIMITIVE MAN, AND MOST OF THE AUTHORITIES I ASKED ABOUT THIS SAID IT WAS PROBABLY BECAUSE WOMEN DIED OF OTHER CANCERS LONG BEFORE THEY REACHED THE VULNERABLE BREAST-CANCER AGE.

You accuse me of rudeness, but how polite is it to stalk a face tutto il girono? I've seen you follow some poor unsuspecting jaw or brow or nose, fixing your eyes upon that arbitrary face until surrender. How many victims, for instance, did you seize in the Borghetto before Judas was filled in? L'Ultima Cena senza l'ultima testa per tanti mesi—ridicolo!

What nerve is the cause of the eye's movement and makes the movement of one eye draw the other?
Of closing the eyelids.
Of raising the eyebrow.
Of lowering the eyebrows.

Try closing one eye and picking a point on an object within two to three feet of you. Now, starting with your finger on the tip of your nose, try to touch the point on the object. Try doing the same thing with both eyes open. In the first case, it's difficult to judge if your finger has traveled far enough or not. In the second case, your finger moves rapidly to the spot without hesitation. The same holds true for similar tasks in the virtual world.

Of shutting the eyes.
Of opening the eyes.

You roll your eyes at me affecting indignation. But we both know I get away with anything—almost. We both know it is our destiny that we be strangely linked, like breath to flame, like hand to kite. Your destiny is to be always seeking flight, and mine: to pull you down to earth, to make you roll in dirt, or worse. This game depends on your participation. You remain eternally enamored of possibility, and I, at every moment, your desire's doubt.

Why as the image of the light of the candle diminishes when it is removed to a great distance from the eye the size of this light does not diminish but it lacks only the power and brightness of this radiance.

The radiologist can alter brightness and contrast, and zoom into specific areas, magnifying as well as reducing image size.

Sometimes I wake to find my master staring over me. I spit on him. Must I endure your probing when I'm still asleep? Couldn't you ask permission? Your face in innocence, he says, is all I wanted, as he sketches, before you distort its sweet natural expression with your vile grimaces. I want to hold the startling beauty of your fair radiant eyes, no less than when the sun from darkness rises. It's too early for poetry, caro Zio, I'll close these heavy lids again and turn my back on you, OK? If you can't bear to leave, just sketch my ass.

Radiologists have been studied for longer than any other defined population to assess the late effects of exposure to ionizing radiations received as a consequence of their occupation.

Of raising the nostrils.
Of parting the lips with teeth clenched.
Of bringing the lips to a point.
Of laughing.
Of wondering.

The most natural of expressions on the mysterious face of the woman on the balcony, do you recall it? I promise I will never tell the world how you contrived it with a band of revelers and musicians in the studio daily provoking Monna Lisa, Francesco del Giocondo's wife, to curve her lips ever so slightly, enigmatically, nearly imperceptibly....And did you finish even so? Four years went by with brush strokes missing from the robes and landscape, left for your pupils to be responsible for—Oh, don't look at me, I wouldn't dare, all are aware I do not work to excellent effect. But don't think I'm complaining, I'd prefer you be occupied with these interminable labors or join her singing revelers than that you serenade me in my bed!

Like the director of a chorus, an MR scanner conducts the "singing" of hydrogen atoms within the human body. The scanner surrounds the body with powerful electromagnets. Supercooled by liquid helium, they create a magnetic field as much as 30,000 times stronger than that of the earth.

Let the earth turn on which side it may the surface of the waters will never move from its spherical form, but will always remain equidistant from the center of the globe. Granting that the earth might be removed from the center of the globe, what would happen to the water?

Couldn't we just once play an ordinary game, as children do?—not a perspectograph, not strange inventions, not artist's tools, not rotting creatures (sempre qualcosa di schifoso), not something to learn from or marvel at—but something simple, divertente, as even my poor father found the time to use with me, and with my sister?

Spinning like tops, the protons normally point in random directions. But inside the scanner's magnetic field they align themselves in the direction of the field's poles. Even in alignment, however, they wobble, or precess, at a specific rate, or frequency. The stronger the magnetic field, the greater the frequency.

In reading right to left his never-ending notes, sometimes with the assistance of a mirror, I feel as when my sister and I would grasp each other's hands and spin around until we were so dizzy we would fall. We laughed then, now I scratch my head and blink instead. Ogni tanto I wonder what would become of little Giacomo were Leonardo suddenly to cease creating. What would my waters have to crash against without his earth?

When the scanner excites these protons with a radio pulse timed to the same frequency as their wobbling, it knocks them out of their alignment.

My master confided to me that as an infant in the cradle he felt the tail of a kite against his lips, and I at a slightly more advanced age often feel the tip of a pen or a silverpoint pencil (it's true I've stolen one or two from other pupils) or brush, always scratching or stroking uncomfortably near to my skin. Absurd, you say, a tactile sense so sensitive, but my master has said, the greater the sensibility the greater the suffering, and I may as well use that to my advantage with him. For the gala festivities of the many pageants he has prepared, Leonardo has created an animated heaven and a cannon that spews forth a flaming actor; for the Masque of the Planets, the first that I observed, he made a giant egg surrounded by signs of the zodiac. In each he tries to include me, put me on display. I do not mind the admiration, for which, in preparation, Leonardo takes his brush and paints my lips; the bristles tickle me.

Cancer therapy can cause dental and oral complications so severe they can compromise cancer treatment and recovery, dental experts said today in recommending that cancer patients get thorough oral examination before treatment.

But other times, art bruises little Giacomo. Cruel master, I am quick to say on these occasions, keep my fine apparel, give me back to poverty. Dove è mio povero padre? Poor father had no soldi, and no schola, not a learned man but decent; at least he left me in peace. Signor Caprotti, tu eri un uomo normale, I miss you! Why did you steal me from him, cradle snatcher? And you call me a thief! Wait...come back. I didn't mean it, master. Please come back and sing to me.

This plan of mine of the human body will be unfolded to you just as though you had the natural man before you. The reason is that if you wish to know thoroughly the parts of a man after he has been dissected you must either turn him or your eye so that you are examining from different aspects, from below, from above and from the sides, turning him over and studying the origin of each limb; and in such a way the natural anatomy has satisfied your desire for knowledge.

Master, put aside your studies; why must you wonder about everything? Come sing to your Salai. Please don't stay away.

The current conventional techniques of 2-D radiation therapy employ multiple radiation fields aimed at the tumor from various angles built in a single plane of the body...With the aid of specialized computer programs, we can precisely reconstruct the 3-D configuration of the tumor, look at it from any side and geometry, define its borders, and determine its relationship to other organs.

BY THIS TIME SOME TINY "GANGS" OF CANCER CELLS HAVE BROKEN AWAY FROM THE ORIGINAL MASS AND HAVE STARTED THRIVING COLONIES IN THE BRAIN AND IN THE LUNGS, PLACES TO WHICH THE "COLONISTS" WERE CARRIED BY THE BLOODSTREAM.

The rumbling of the cannon is caused by the impetuous fury of the flame beaten back by the resisting air, and that quantity of the powder causes this effect because it finds itself ignited within the body of the cannon; and not perceiving itself in a place that has capacity for it to increase, nature guides it to search with fury for a place suitable for its increase, and breaking or driving before it the weaker obstacle it wins its way into the spacious air; and this not being capable of escaping with the speed with which it is attacked, because the fire is more volatile than the air....

The Department of Defense has long used image enhancement in evaluating aerial pictures in camouflage detection, and more recently this equipment has been applied in medical imaging.

Kaposi's sarcoma, it turned out, was probably the most important single clue to the discovery of AIDS in New York in 1981, and it remains an integral part of the baffling investigation of its cause, cure and prevention.

Crossbows, catapults, chariots with scythes, cannonballs, bombs, and one life-like dove bobbing from a string: charming designs, indeed, master. But what are these words beside them? I must as usual apply the mirror to decode... Madonna, can it be...could he be addressing me? I want no more war with you, Salai.

The original technology for sound imaging came from defense department research in underwater sonar dating back to 1942, and even earlier when airborne radar was developed in the 30's.

How by a certain machine many may stay some time under water. And how and wherefore I do not describe my method of remaining under water and how long I can remain without eating. And I do not publish nor divulge these, by reason of the evil nature of men, who would use them for assassinations at the bottom of the sea by destroying ships, and sinking them, together with the men in them.

How strange to hear you droning "Mangia, mangia" instead of "Basta, Salai. Basta!" Today—non so perché—I have no appetite. Perhaps it was our session with the putrid corpse, those hours diagramming all that nature in her wisdom hides inside.

Describe all the heights and breadths of the intestines, and measure them by fingers in halves and thirds of fingers of a dead man's hand, and for all put at what distance they are from the navel the breasts or flanks of the dead.

Instead of the common method of introducing an opaque barium liquid into the gastrointestinal tract, Laufer has his patients swallow effervescent granules that produce gas. Then the barium is introduced. As the barium passes from the system some of it outlines the intestinal tract to define the folds of the structure. Films obtained by this method reveal much greater contour and detail than those obtained using barium mixtures alone.

What kind of household is this anyway?: a man who draws incessantly, dissects dead bodies day and night, and since I arrived has divided his spare time between creating all the props for the Castello Sforzesco's Masque of the Planets and assembling a giant bronze horse to honor the Duke of Milan. He will teach me all he knows, he claims, and he knows more than anyone I've ever met, but do I want to learn it? The war is on, it cannot be ignored, and Italy must fortify itself against superior French artillery. Therefore, your horse, Leonardo, that is to say, your plans and molds and casts, are useless. Your seventy-two tons of bronze is only cannon fodder now: your noble head and mighty haunches, the sleek enormity of your gran cavallo, is just a heap of shit. Watch it depart in one brown lump upon the barge, off to Ferrara to be converted into something useful.

In countries like Japan and China and among vegetarian groups, cholesterol levels and colon cancer rates are very low.

Do I recall your own distinction: some men merely fill latrines, those, I presume, who don't make art. But sometimes art might just as well be shit, ho ragione? Your horse, your birds that do not fly, all shit on you.

The frog retains life for some hours when the head the heart and all the intestines have been taken away. And if you prick the cord it instantly twitches and dies. All the nerves of the animals derive from here: when this is pricked it instantly dies...

I WAS NOT EXAMINING MYSELF FOR SUSPECTED CANCER. ALL I WAS DOING WAS SHAVING UNDER MY ARM. SOMEHOW THE LITTLE FINGER OF THE HAND THAT HELD THE RAZOR LEAPFROGGED OVER

How the nerves sometimes act of themselves without the command of other functions of the mind. This is clearly apparent for you will see paralytics, cowards and the benumbed move their trembling members, such as the head or hands, without permission of the mind.

Holding up your gloved hand in front of you, you would see a simple, blocky, wire-frame representation of a hand. You could turn it and move your fingers, and the disembodied hand would mimic the motion. Using fiberoptic sensors to measure the flex of each finger joint and an additional position and orientation sensor, the computer knew exactly where your hand was and what movements your fingers made.

Months after concern over the spread of the AIDS virus caused a shortage of rubber gloves, a New Britain-based medical supplier is stuck with millions of them.

She put the scalpel on a tray and, moments later, the instruments sliced a three-millimeter hole in Dr. Dressner's gloved finger as she reached for a catheter.

The mind with all its powers cannot prevent these members from trembling. This also happens in epilepsy and in members which have been severed, as in the tails of lizards.

O Leonardo, I applaud you; Salai is entertained by your tamed and decorated lizard from the garden, with his quicksilver scales, beard, wings and big eyes. Open the box's lid once more; let's scare another unsuspecting passerby! I like those horns best of all; did you fashion them in my honor: il tuo piccolo diabolo? When your father saw the shield that depicted your first demon beast, he begged Verrochio to take you on. But my father made no such request. You conned him to surrender me. Was that smart, master? You are supposed to be wise, but sometimes I could swear that only height persuades the onlooker that you are man and I am child.

A man at three years will have reached the half of his height.
A woman of the same size as a man will weigh less than he does.
A dead woman lies face downwards in water, a man the opposite way.

The worldwide AIDS epidemic is gaining momentum and in some regions has shifted from a disease mostly among men to one in which half the victims are women, officials of the World Health Organization said today.
Do you think that you, a mortal man, can conquer God's ravages: this plague, it has been said, his wrath upon Milano, although strange so swiftly was it purged in Firenze. Perhaps you will produce your sanitation plans in verse, as you wash the streets with paddle wheels. Hygiene for cities would be a splendid title. Render poetic your references to herds of humans breeding pestilence. We should not be atop one another, compassionate master architect/designer/engineer declares. And so you make two cities, in your pretty, refined plans (complete with chimneys, spiral stairs, canals and swiveling privy seats), one atop the other, the gentlemen above, the artisans below; but Leonardo, where does that leave us, we are on bottom with the beasts, the animals whom you adore and would not eat now also keep our company? Shall we all dine together on verdure?

The study involved 750 Italian women. Those who ate the most fats, saturated fats and animal protein had a three times greater chance of getting breast cancer than those whose intake of these foods was lowest.

Finish my plate? It's true, I usually finish two. And you, master, no meat, again? Does it not weaken you, this diet of funghi, minestrone, insalata? Is meat too sensual: abbacchio, bistecca et vitello, like velvet in your mouth, on your tongue? Would that disturb you? Or is la carne less compelling than your precious decomposing creatures in the back room, about whom no one ever asked Salai, "do they disturb you, dear?"

You will begin at the rectum and enter on the left side of the colon, but first elevate the bone of the pubis and of the flanks (ilium) with a chisel the better to observe the position of the intestines.

One of the greatest challenges facing a world designer lies in creating the 3-D models needed for building virtual experiences. Because of performance constraints (the update rate decreases as the number of polygons increases), world designers have to carefully construct their world—too many polygons and it becomes jerky and uninhabitable.

Were I to emulate my master perfectly, I'd soon address the king— write him a humble letter of introduction listing my accomplishments. "O king," I'd begin cleverly, "I'm ever so busy at the moment but if you beg me on your regal knees there is the slightest chance I could be persuaded to be at your service. And did I mention, suddenly I've become proficient at making every imaginable implement of destruction?" Perhaps I'd dabble in Arabic as well and write the Sultan with an offer to build a bridge linking Istanbul to Pera. Why not be an engineer this week? Better still, a military engineer! Make bombs and guns and fortresses though hitherto, admittedly, I have been occupied exclusively with painting saints and angels!

All the spiritual powers, in proportion as they are farther away from their primary or secondary cause, occupy more space and become of less potency.

Before you ever thought of planning cities, you immortalized the rocks and trees. I hasten to assure you that your landscape honors nature in her beauty. Its rhythms are so intricate as to inspire awe. It is the first ever drawn, I understand. But master, can a mountain commission its portrait? Does a tree possess the vanity to pose? (Perhaps you, vegetarian, imagine so?—that all things sense.) Your struggle was confirmed from your first drawing then. You are no penny painter, you complain, yet you are always crying soldi, soldi! Don't be so spoiled; for once humble yourself to flatter the rich as an artisan should. Humor Isabella d'Este with a portrait. Or a Virgin or a Christchild, anything! If you were only practical, I wouldn't have to steal!

A leaf always turns its upper side towards the sky so that it may the better receive, on all its surface, the dew which drops gently from the atmosphere. And these leaves are so distributed on the plant as that one shall cover the other as little as possible, but shall lie alternately one above another as may be seen in the ivy which covers the walls.

This baffle system is placed between the x-ray source and the patient. "Up to 80 leaves guided by motors can duplicate any tumor in size and shape," Dr. Fuks further explained.

Using a trick developed by the flight-simulation industry, two intersecting polygons and the transparent texture of a tree can be combined to form a very realistic 3-D image of a tree, as illustrated in Fig. 6-10. If you're building a virtual forest with hundreds of trees, tricks like this are crucial to creating a sense of realism with only a few polygons to go around.

Provocation is my only weapon against his calm certainty. His catapults and cannons do not move me, but the spew of his words, his scrutiny of everything exhausts, invades, it overwhelms me. Each item in the universe is marked with his curiosity, and they mount to make an impenetrable fortress of his creativity. Solve for me this riddle, per piacere: is my master every creature's lover, or a dog who needs to piss on every tree?

Why is the fish in the water swifter than the bird in the air when it ought to be the contrary seeing that the water is heavier and thicker than the air and the fish is heavier and has smaller wings than the bird?

If a kite came to me in my sleep I would grab onto its tail and hope to sail from this madness. Better still, we could all of us in Italia flap kites in each hand and the whole of humanity fly above Leonardo's ingenious second level: this would alleviate the overcrowding in Milano and all of the cities; a third tier would be introduced to the design and the foul vapor of plague would never reach us in the air! Sto scherzando.

This, being evacuated every day by the mesaraic portal, is deposited in the bowels causing the same stench when it has reached there as arises from all the dead in the sepulchers, and this is the stench of the feces.

Must he always organize and itemize, even fantasize constructively? His pages filled with idle scribbles ask for violation; I have no choice but to steal glances at my master's private writings if I am to do my job. Oggi: uno sguardo di nascosto: With pencil he has made an articulated sphincter blossom into a fleur de lis which in turn becomes a fortress of five sides. You mustn't pick those petals Leonardo, vietato!
But in your dreams? Do you create fiori in the night? And do they cause in you while you sleep the same motion below as takes place in the hung man?

Definition of a sphincter by puckering of the skin, that is, the eyes, nares, mouth, vulva, penis and anus.

On this folio, your bicycle invention is neighbored by a huge, walking, tail-wagging cazzo, aiming itself toward a circle who some smart-ass apprentice has beneath it labeled....S-A-L- ... Who has printed my name? Who has dared to name this hole Salai?

The stone thrown into the water becomes the center of various circles, and these have as their center the spot which has been struck.

Your imagination, master, is prodigious, your fantasies outlandish, but this useless list of Latin words and your assiduous study of mathematics are frankly dubious. Concentrate now on the simple tallying, as often your relentless record keeping ends in error. Questo e ironico, no? Lunedì: connect Florence to the sea by canal, Martedì: make a bridge between Europe and Asia, and while you're at it, devise flight for a man from the wing of a bat. Però, when you add up the household needs you arrive at a ludicrous sum! Think hard now, Leonardo, what is one plus one?

CANCER IS THE RESULT OF ONE OR MORE CELLULAR MUTATIONS OR OTHER PERSISTENT CHANGES IN THE CONTROL OF GENETIC EXPRESSION. THIS IS THE ONLY WAY TO EXPLAIN WHY, WHEN A CANCER CELL DIVIDES, THE RESULT IS TWO CANCER CELLS.

And the air in the same way is filled with circles, the centers of which are the sounds and voices formed within them.

Master, what's a boy to do with rumors that have currency of plague? No, perfumed hanky can protect me from the gossip of the streets. I cannot plug my ears. Is it not true that your master Verrochio in his adolescence killed a fourteen year old boy when he carelessly threw a stone, and that he should have gone to prison, but was released because his case was unoriginal? (The same Verrochio, by the way, with whom you stayed four extra years when it was obvious to all that you were more than ready to embark upon your own career. What kept you there?)

A New York State AIDS panel today criticized the refusal of prison authorities to provide prisoners with condoms to prevent infection, saying the policy "amounts to a death sentence."

That trial seems not unlike your own, Zio Leonardo, so the Florentines have told the Milanese, for a crime at least as unoriginal as injuries attributable to careless stones, with one Jacobo Sartorelli, the man who dressed in black, who did his goldsmithing by day and di notte un altro lavoro—but lacked, of course, a brothel; hence my master would not likely have visited his residence to draw the boy who dressed in black while you in pink...

FINALLY, SEXUAL ACTIVITY IS A HIGHLY CHARGED, INTERPERSONAL MIX OF PHYSICAL PLEASURE AND COMPLEX PSYCHOLOGICAL STATES. ACCORDINGLY, PERSUASION OR COERCION, PHYSICAL ATTRACTION OR DESIRE, AND EMOTIONAL BONDS OR NEEDS EXERT A POWERFUL INFLUENCE OVER EROTIC CONDUCT.

And the heart though it is not made of skin.

Unsafe Practices
Downloading of software from bulletin board systems
Using public domain software (shareware)
Using pirated or illegitimate copies of software
Using computer games...
Booting up from the diskette drive (A:drive)

And can you explain this torn sheet dated 1478: 'Fioravante di Domenico in Firenze is my most cherished companion, as though he were my...' Who is, or was, more cherished by Leonardo than his Salai? Perhaps your newer apprentice Melzi, for that matter. The ever-reliable Melzi, always at your beck and call. Whose wealthy parents have a fine estate where you can stay, who does not need assistance for his sister's dowry. As does Salai.

If the object of love is worthless,
the lover cheapens himself.

SHE IS APT TO FEEL LESS FEMININE, LESS SEXY, UGLY, AND SO ON, AND TO PASS THIS DROP IN SELF-ESTEEM ALONG TO HER HUSBAND AND CHILDREN. ASKEN CALLS IT A "DISTORTED SELF VIEW AS A PERSON UNWORTHY AND UNABLE TO READAPT TO HER NORMAL ROLE."

In death you left me only half a vineyard and the house I built. What did Melzi receive?

FOR EXAMPLE, THE INFLUENCE OF A SEXUAL PARTNER CAN UNDERMINE AN INDIVIDUAL'S ATTEMPT TO PRACTICE SAFER SEX AND PROMPT HIM TO ENGAGE IN RISKY CONDUCT. SIMILARLY, THE POWERFUL DRIVES ASSOCIATED WITH LOVE, AFFECTION, AND DESIRE CAN FOSTER FURTHER EPISODES OF RISK BEHAVIOR.

Leonardo, have you heard the latest about your fellow bastard, Cesare Borgia? Your friend murders whom he chooses, stabs his own brother, has relations with his sister—oh, do I offend you to mention these unpleasant matters? All that truly matters is that he favors you and your Machiavelli. It seems you'll stoop to anything to gain a title. Military Engineer!

The change in the heart at its death is similar to the change which it makes during the expulsion of blood, and is a little less. This is shown when one sees the pigs in Tuscany where they pierce the hearts of the pigs by means of an instrument called a spile with which wine is drawn from casks. And so, after turning the pig over and having tied it up well, they pierce its right side together with its heart by means of this spile, thrusting it straight inwards. If the spile passes through the heart when it is elongated, the heart in shortening itself on the expulsion of its blood draws the wound upwards together with the point of the spile.

"There's blood flying, needles flying," he said. "You can't be absolutely careful in the emergency room unless you're not going to take the best care of the patient."

Stress was induced by an injection of dipyradamole, which simulates exercise by boosting blood flow to healthy muscle tissues. The increased flow, however, is blocked by an artery with a constriction.

You make every day a party, master. Blowing with your secret blacksmith's bellows the hollowed sheep's intestine until it fills the room. Now that's a fine impressive balloon! All the squeamish gentlemen and ladies shrink and tremble in the corners in terror of a vast inflated gut! Whoopee! Do it again. Facciamolo ancora!

The outer catheter is pulled back and the balloon is inflated until it compresses the materials clogging the artery and again allows the blood to supply the heart muscle.

But painting with food at the Casa Martelli is even more fun. Where else could a boy learn to make a Virgin Mary out of cheese, or a landscape whose trees are constructed of sausage and jelly?

This could be something merely prankish, such as displaying a message or a bouncing dot on the screen. Unfortunately, it is often something more pernicious, such as damaging or destroying data, programs, the operating system, or even attached peripherals.

The colon and the other intestines become greatly contracted in the aged, and I have found there stones in the vessels which pass beneath the clavicles of the chest. These were as large as chestnuts, of the color and shape of truffles or of dross or clinkers of iron. These stones were extremely hard, like these clinkers, and had formed sacs attached to the said vessels, in the manner of goiters.

Sticks and stones can break my bones but names can never hurt me. Or can they? Sometimes? Bastardo, bastardo. Da Vinci, il bastardo. How about the name Michelangelo? A man of noble lineage; in somma, NOT a bastard, not a scribbler, not a dabbler, but a real poet, who has been given the wall across from your blank battle of Anghiari for his Battle of Cascina. He's only twenty-nine, isn't he? But old enough to remember that you voted against his statue of David being displayed in the piazza. Si, lo so, you wished it be protected from the weather. Non ci credo!

One use of Doppler is diagnosing an embolism or occlusion of an artery in a patient who has had a stroke. Irregular pressures and flow patterns result just as if a rock had broken loose and was disrupting the flow of a stream.

Piove, piove, che strano, che male. It's raining whips and helmets; it's raining stools and compasses. It's raining rakes and caldrons and lanterns. Bizzarro. What strange hail you're making, what strange things you're drawing. Calm down now. Con calma. Go and make an olive press. Go and make a candelabrum. Go invent a mirror with eight sides, a fortress with five sides. Con calma. Be rid of these visions. Be rid of this nightmare.

In the unstressed heart the scanner shows white and orange where absorption of the radioisotope is greatest. But in the heart under stress there is only yellow in its upper half, indicating a partial blockage in the coronary artery feeding that part of the heart. left untreated, this defect may eventually cause a heart attack. Deteted by the PET scanner, it could be prevented.

The problems with paint, with surface, with....quasi-fresco, they could have been—had you only known—had you only thought, only tested, been more focused on the single task at hand—-had you only... paid attention!

As each of us gradually gives up the inborn certainty of our physical immortality, we hope to die of old age very quickly and in full control of our faculties up to the last minute. "Let it be anything but cancer."

The time it takes to develop AIDS after being infected with the virus is longer than previously estimated, a new study indicates.

And this old man, a few hours before his death, told me that he had passed one hundred years, and that he was conscious of no failure of body, except feebleness. And thus sitting upon a bed in the hospital of Santa Maria Nuova in Florence, without any untoward movement or sign, he passed from this life. And I made an anatomy to see the cause of death so sweet...

Most of the caregivers were forced to deal with their grief in an abrupt manner. One father described how he was forced to face this fact: "I was sitting with my son. I must have looked really depressed or something, because he all of a sudden said 'Hey, dad! C'mon. I'm not dead yet. Don't bury me till I am.'" The young man here had just recovered from his fifth bout of PCP (pneumocystis carinii pneumonia), demonstrating the increasing chronicity of AIDS.

This anatomy I described very carefully and with great ease owing to the absence of fat and humor which rather hinder recognition of the parts. The other anatomy was that of a child of two years in which I found everything to be the opposite to that of the old man.

Responding to the arrests Sunday of more than one hundred people protesting his statements on homosexuality, AIDS and abortion, John Cardinal O'Connor said yesterday that his approach could be changed only 'over my dead body'...

write what the soul is

Anyone superstitious? In 1503, on the day of the move from Santa Maria Novella to the council chamber of the Palazzo Vecchio, the rains came, your paints ran, the vessel burst, your fire was too far to dry .... you failed, you failed again, the cartoon of the Battle of Anghiari tore. The rains came down, the sun never shone through the dark day. No wonder you grow weary of the brush. Non lo finirai mai. Piove, piove... da Vinci non vince.

The heart is of such density that fire can scarcely damage it. This is seen in the case of men who have been burnt, in whom after their bones are in ashes the heart is still bloody internally.

Checking for bone density loss in post menopausal women, a spinal bone scan can reveal the possible risk of fractures. The monitor indicates only minor risk in this patient. Screening for osteoporosis in women older than 51 years uses this nuclear medicine technique.

Sticks and stones can break my bones but my master can saw them asunder to see if they be hollow, even a skull he can.

Needle sticks are believed to be the most common way that health care workers get AIDS virus infections on the job, but the infection has been passed by contaminated blood through mucous membranes lining the eyes, nose and mouth, said an editorial accompanying the article.

The most common procedure in the department is a full-body bone scan done with a single plane gamma camera using technetium 99m tagged to phosphonates as the radionuclide tracer. Once injected, it travels to and is absorbed by the bones of the entire skeleton.

How pretty are the shadows of the contour of the skull—normally discreetly hidden—my master hollows for the viewer's eye to see. (But here's a hint: if master were to craft a key to lock me in my room, I wage a bet that here is where my room would be.) Yes, I could happily reside in such a handsome cavity: a voice ensconced in darkness.

The idea or imagination is the helm or bridle of the sense, for the thing imagined moves the senses.
To pre-imagine is to imagine things which will be.
To post-imagine is to imagine things past.

He can measure the length of our interior passageways and the bulk of their unsavory contents, the depth of a woman's womb, the throbbing of a heart or a cock, but tell me, Uncle Leonardo, what are the facts of life? A child can't understand these treatises and diagrams. Just translate to a language I can understand. Madonna, someone tell me what is going on inside my little trembling sausage?

Of the virile member when it is hard, it is thick and long, dense and heavy, and when it is limp, it is thin, short and soft, that is, limp and weak. This should not be adjudged as due to the addition of flesh or wind, but to arterial blood. I have seen this in the dead who have this member rigid. For many die thus, especially those hanged of whom I have seen an anatomy, having great density and hardness, and these are full of a large quantity of blood which has made the flesh very red within, and in others, without as well as within.

BUT DESPITE THE SUBSTANTIAL NUMBER OF COUPLES THAT HAD RECENTLY TALKED ABOUT CONDOMS, FEW AGREEMENTS TO USE THEM RESULTED. NEGOTIATIONS RAISED SENSITIVE ISSUES OF LOYALTY, TRUST, CONTROL AND SEXUAL PERFORMANCE — ISSUES THAT THREATENED TO AFFECT THE STATUS QUO IN RELATIONSHIPS AND CAUSE MAJOR DISRUPTIONS.

I know how master gets erect: from observing the erection of a man with a rope about his neck. The tighter the noose, the stiffer the....Now don't forget your pen! Excuse me, could you hold that pose a moment longer? Che peccatto! He may not have finished Mona Lisa's vestita but this sketch of the condemned will have utmost fidelity to the fox fur on the blue cloak, the blue serge jerkin, the red and black velvet bands of his any-minute-superfluous collar.

FOR EXAMPLE, NINE WOMEN WHO HAVE RAISED THE ISSUE OF CONDOMS MENTIONED THAT THEIR PARTNERS ACCUSED THEM OF HAVING AIDS. NEGOTIATING CONDOM USE WITH PARTNERS PROVED TO BE MORE THAN A MATTER OF "COMMUNICATION SKILLS."

A WNBC-TV crew walked off the set at a Manhattan studio yesterday rather than tape an interview with two victims of AIDS, station officials said.

Safe practices
Using anti-virus software
Using only shrink-wrapped software from a reputable vendor
Write protecting software when possible (for example, using write protect tabs on original diskettes)
Making regular backups according to a carefully designed system...

The origin of the penis is situated upon the pubic bone so that it can resist its active force on coition. If this bone did not exist, the penis in meeting resistance would turn backwards and would often enter more into the body of the operator than into that of the operated.

Master, your Salai was never one to beat around the bush: is your slowness due to hours spent in idle self-abuse among the rotting bodies? Or inside them? Do you make a puppet of your penis for this private pageant?
You look alarmed, disturbed. Che c'è? Has il ragazzo cattivo gone finally too far with his insouciance? Suddenly it's dark, there's no time to answer. Sta piovendo, guarda, it's raining whips and helmets and floating beds and tables, and foxes, snakes and lions; our hands cover our eyes, then our throats, a man's hands make a vase for his neck, children are struck by their mothers to save them from dying a worse death. It's raining dark and frantic. Collapsing mountains, trees uprooted, corpses strewn like seaweed. The winds so strong with rain and hail, the sea so rough. Aiuto!

The fullness of the rectum, being dense, is expelled entirely by the wind contained in the colon. All the faeces of which the

intestines empty themselves, are almost entirely driven out by this wind. This causes a noise when it is in excess following the filling up of the vacuum left by the aforementioned superfluities.

You badger me with your charity, bore me with your disappointment in my skills, assault me daily with your insatiable imagination, why don't you just bugger me and get it done with! That's what everyone assumes already anyway.

The boy was later freed. He ran to school and told a security guard what had happened...The police arrested a suspect who, they said later, was infected with the virus that causes AIDS.

The same will be found at the mouth of the penis, of the vulva and of the womb, and all structures which receive necessary things and expel the superfluous.

Mayor Edward I. Koch, who joined the Cardinal at the party yesterday, called the protest an "excrescence."

Since Dr. Kaposi's time, doctors have described lesions that grew large enough to block the intestines. Such a complication can be fatal if surgery is not performed immediately.

Perhaps you too will die a filler of latrines. And O but what a fine latrine whose seat can swivel on a counterweight. More practical than a monstrous bucking bronze! Surely the stuff of immortality! To impress the Duke, you offered him a marvelous silver lyre, shaped as a horse's head, for all to marvel at. But master, so fond of mirror tricks, take a suggestion from your humble apprentice: It would be far more clever still to turn that lyre around, then instantly you've made a mirror! Affanculo, Leonardo, you're a horse's ass.

The images of the surrounding things are transmitted to the senses, and the senses transmit them to the organ of perception, and the organ of perception transmits them to the common sense, and by it they are imprinted on the memory, and are retained there more or less distinctly according to the importance or power of the thing given.

"YOUR SENSATION WILL GRADUALLY RETURN. DON'T WORRY," DR.
DAO ASSURED ME. WHAT HE DID NOT EXPLAIN WAS THAT WHEN THE
SENSATION CAME BACK, IT WOULD COME AS PAIN.

*If you're no penny painter, master, why can you still not obtain
enough commissions to keep a big fat purse? Why are you wander-
ing around the Sistine Chapel looking lost—and toward the end of
your career without a painting underway and with a salary of only
33 ducats a month? Never mind what Raphael received for every
room. (Well, if you must know, twelve thousand.)*

*An image obtained by using single photon emission computed tomography
(SPECT) shows a patch of darkness in the brain of a 57 year old man.
Reflecting a decrease in blood flow to the parietal lobes—where sensation from
the eyes and ears are associated with memory—darkness symbolizes the
agony of Alzheimer's disease.*

*"The first experimenters had great concerns about what the magnet might do
to humans", Dr. Worthington recalled. "I remember someone questioning
whether we might even remove centers of memory in the brain with too strong
a magnet."*

"THE FIRST COUPLE OF YEARS, THE OPERATION IS REMEMBERED AS
EXCRUCIATING. THEN IT DIMINISHES TO VERY PAINFUL. THEN,
SOMEWHERE ALONG THE LINE, THE 'VERY' DISAPPEARS, AND ULTI-
MATELY A MASTECTOMY IS REMEMBERED ONLY AS UNCOMFORTABLE
AND EVEN ALTOGETHER PAIN-FREE."

*Master, must there be so many mirrors here in our last years
together? I see us everywhere I step, you and I and Melzi, there are
so many of us everywhere, as if our phantom bodies propagated end-
lessly in glass.*

In an anatomy, with all your ability, you will not see and will not
obtain knowledge except of a few vessels, to acquire a true and
full knowledge of which I have dissected more than ten human
bodies, destroying every other member and removing in very
minute particles all the flesh which surrounded these vessels with-

out causing them to bleed except for the insensible bleeding of
the capillary vessels.

EVEN MORE RARELY DO WE QUESTION THE ABILITY OF SCIENCE TO KNOW.

*The expertise of the radiation oncologist lies in his knowledge of the best
method of treatment for a specific tumor in a specific location. Among many
other things, he must decide on total dose, time of delivery, amount and kind
of radiation (electron, photon, neutron or proton), possible harm to surrounding tissue areas, and expected tumor response.*

*One of Barbara Bush's doctors said today that the dosage of her eye medication
had been altered and that radiation therapy was being considered.*

FOR THE MOST PART, SCIENCE SERVES AS THE MASTER DISCOURSE
THAT ADMINISTERS ALL OTHER DISCOURSES ABOUT AIDS.

*Many people think a film has a definitive answer, only one answer. This is
not true.*

*Martina Navratilova said she believes the public's response would have
been much different if it had been her and not Magic Johnson who announced
a positive test for the virus that causes AIDS.*

ALTHOUGH SCIENCE IS OFTEN NOT SPECIFICALLY REFERENCED, THE
COMMON ASSUMPTION UNDERLYING DEBATES ON PUBLIC POLICY
OR THE VOICING OF PERSONAL VIEWS ABOUT SAFER SEX, IS THAT SCI-
ENCE CAN, ULTIMATELY, ANSWER ANY TROUBLING QUESTIONS.

*Q Mr. President, turn your attention to a matter that's devastating here at
home, and all over the world, the question of AIDS.*

*If the average person does not avail himself of someone who understands all
the subtleties in dealing with prostate cancer and does not inform himself properly, then he cannot get proper treatment.*

"RIGHT NOW, ALL I CAN SAY IS THAT A RESEARCH HOSPITAL IS THE
BEST PLACE FOR ME. THEY'VE GOT THE BEST." CLEARLY, HE DID-

N'T AGREE. "IT'S YOUR BODY," HE SAID. "WHATEVER YOU SAY."

KNOWLEDGE IS PERCEIVED TO ARISE FROM SCIENCE AND FILTER OUT INTO THE SOCIAL AND IMAGINARY WORLD — KNOWLEDGE ABOUT SURVIVING WITH A CHRONIC ILLNESS, ABOUT REINVENTING SEXUAL PLEASURE IN A DISASTER ZONE…

"What is happening with New York's health care? Are we going to be stepping over bodies, like Calcutta?"

A. I spoke at an international AIDS conference at which I was roundly booed two years ago or so, advocating a certain—certain kinds of testing. And I don't want to have—you said mandatory? For everybody?

A single body was insufficient for so long a time, so that it was necessary to proceed by degrees with as many bodies as would give me complete knowledge.

…the last surviving sibling of former President Jimmy Carter, has been found to be suffering from pancreatic cancer, the same disease that killed their father, sister and brother and contributed to the death of their mother.

CONSIDER A GAY MALE NURSE: AT WORK HE IS TOLD HE CAN'T GET AIDS, AT THE BAR HE IS TOLD HE HAD BETTER TAKE EXTRAORDINARY PRECAUTIONS OR HE WILL GET AIDS.

She plans to eventually, but it is not a priority. "I can't test myself after every exposure," Dr. Dressner said.

This I repeated twice in order to see the differences.

… BUT IT IS THE LOGIC OF SCIENCE THAT ANCHORS THE POWER RELATIONS WHICH DETERMINE WHOSE KNOWLEDGE COUNTS AS "REAL," AS "OBJECTIVE."

YOU must know where to go. YOU must do this research.

"This isn't the Kaposi's sarcoma I see in Lusaka. Don't the Americans

know how to treat it?

Q. Mr. President, back to China.

SCIENTISTS RARELY EVEN NEED TO TESTIFY IN POLICY DEBATE BECAUSE SCIENTIFIC THOUGHT MODALITIES HAVE LONG BEEN POP-ULARIZED AND ALREADY UNDERPIN THE STRUCTURE OF THINKING IN THE SOCIAL AND POLITICAL SPHERE.

Q. Mr President, first at the great risk of appearing to be trying to make points, please convey birthday wishes to Mrs. Bush.

... when the President's wife Nancy Reagan was diagnosed as having breast cancer after a routine mammogram, one breast imaging clinic reported a 50% increase in patients requesting the screening.

WE APPROACH THE END OF THE TWENTIETH CENTURY, NOT SO MUCH AS "TECHNOLOGICAL MAN," ROBBED OF EMOTIONALITY AND CULTURAL DEPTH, BUT AS CYBORGS FOR WHOM SCIENCE IS OUR CUL-TURE, OUR MODE OF CONSTRUCTING IDENTITY.

INTRODUCING MYSELF QUICKLY, I TOLD HIM WHY I WAS CALLING. "I'M NOT A KOOK," I SAID, CONVINCINGLY, I HOPE. "I'VE JUST HAD A MASTECTOMY MYSELF, AND I WANT TO PASS ALONG TO THE PRESIDENT SOME OF THE INFORMATION I'VE LEARNED."

Although human ingenuity in various inventions corresponds with various instruments to the same end, it will never find an invention more beautiful, more simple or more direct than does nature, because in her inventions nothing is superfluous.

Consequently, it says, blood should be treated as a toxic substance in the same way that industrial poisons are treated as dangerous chemicals.

In a strange twist of events, equipment once used to create the mind-boggling effects for movies such as George Lucas' Star Wars is now being used to save human lives.

THIS WAS A SITUATION IN WHICH ANY KIND OF SPEECH RECOG-
NIZABLE AS OPERATING WITHIN THE DISCOURSE OF UNITARY OR OF
NETWORK POWER WAS CAPTURED BY SCIENCE, THE MEDIA, THE
POLITICIANS.

*Mr. Petrelis said that even though Phillip Morris had contributed tens of
millions of dollars over the years to artistic programs, its support of Senator
Helms was undermining the good will that had been created.*

THE ONLY REMAINING FORM OF SPEAKING WAS THAT WHICH FELL
BETWEEN THE LEGITIMATED DISCOURSES, SOMETHING APPROACH-
ING THE DISCOURSE OF ART, BUT AN ART OF THE BODY IN
RESISTANCE.

I WAS SPEECHLESS. I FINALLY BLURTED OUT, "THE PRESIDENT HAS
MADE HIS DECISION? IT'S NOT HIS DECISION TO MAKE. MRS. FORD
SHOULD MAKE THAT DECISION, DON'T YOU THINK?"

*Museums, galleries and other arts organizations plan to darken their galleries,
temporarily remove or cover artworks, hold memorial services, or sponsor per-
formances, lectures and exhibitions about AIDS. Some galleries plan to close.*

And if you have a love for such things, you will perhaps be hindered by your stomach, and if this does not prevent you, you may
perhaps be deterred by the fear of living during the night in the
company of quartered and flayed corpses, horrible to see.

Are we going to be stepping over bodies, like Calcutta?

If this does not deter you, perhaps you lack the good draftsmanship which appertains to such demonstrations, and if you
have the draftsmanship, it will not be accompanied by a knowledge of perspective.

AN IMPORTANT THEME IN THE HISTORY OF MEDICINE AND IN
MEDICAL SOCIOLOGY HAS BEEN THAT DISEASES ARE SOCIALLY CON-
STRUCTED ENTITIES, NOT SIMPLY BIOLOGICAL PHENOMENA...

BY ALL MEANS, A MAN MUST GO OUT OF HIS WAY TO SHOW THAT,
WHATEVER PHYSICAL DIFFERENCE THE MASTECTOMY HAS MADE, IT
HAS NOT CHANGED HIS FEELINGS.

*"There is no cure other than to stop the gays. Homosexuality must be outlawed,
or else death will spread like wildfire."*

If it were so accompanied, you lack the methods of geometric
demonstration and the method of calculation of the forces and
power of the muscles. Perhaps you lack the patience so that
you will not be diligent. Whether all these qualities were found
in me or not, the hundred and twenty books composed by me will
supply the verdict, yes or no.

*Mr. Koch, in a statement, said the flier was "vicious, malicious and intended
to harm me politically."*

ONE ASPECT OF THE SOCIAL CONSTRUCTION OF AIDS THAT
AFFECTS PATIENTS' EXPERIENCE INVOLVES DISEASE DEFINITIONS
THAT ARE, TO SOME EXTENT, MEDICALLY ARBITRARY.

"I can get rid of Kaposi's. They must be using the wrong drugs."

THE EFFECT OF SUCH DEFINITIONS IS PARTICULARLY IMPORTANT
IN A POLITICAL CULTURE IN WHICH THE PROVISION AND FINANC-
ING OF HEALTH CARE IS PARTICULARISTIC RATHER THAN
UNIVERSAL, WHERE ACCESS TO BENEFITS AND CARE SYSTEMS
DEPENDS ON SUCH SPECIFIC CHARACTERISTICS OF THE INDIVID-
UAL AS EMPLOYMENT, FAMILY, DISABILITY, OR INCOME STATUS.

"Then," she said, "things changed dramatically in 1983."

*The National Institutes of Health want to break the monopoly on supply
of the AIDS drug AZT in hopes that competition will lower the price, officials said today.*

"IF THE PRESIDENT'S WIFE ISN'T GOING TO GET THE BEST," I
ASKED, "WHO IS?"

"The attitude they have is that you're dying so why should they put their best forward," said Evelyn B., a 39-year-old woman with HIV, the virus that causes AIDS.

IT IS LITTLE COMFORT TO KNOW THAT DEATH IS PART OF THE NATURAL ORDER; THAT DYING HAS BEEN GOING ON FOREVER, THAT WE WILL ALL DIE EVENTUALLY.

In these pursuits I have been hindered by neither avarice nor by negligence but only by lack of time.

Your words, master, begin to blur before me. I hear your voice in altered form, as if you spoke from under water. What will there be for me to hold onto if you abandon me? I am too young, I am too old. I sense I am almost alone.

Farewell.

Here at St. Florentin of Amboise, what remains? Sticks and stones like scattered bones whose name is never certain. Buried once, buried twice, unmarked graves removed in order to repair a chateau, and so as to leave the view unobstructed by unsightly tombs: a landscape such as one could draw.
Here at the cemetery of the collegiate Church of St. Florentin, time, without the assistance of sized silk or lime-strengthened pine or feathered canvas, without the assistance of harness or rudder or cables or platform, takes wing, embracing us or striking us? Suffocating? A dragon or a swan or a kite? Chi sa quale? Make a fine fist to grab hold of the kite's fierce tail. Then release it and rest at last.

Master, paint the convent clock or we will have no meat. Time is flying.

The air is full of an infinite number of images of the things which are distributed through it, and all of these are represented in all, all in one, and all in each. Consequently it so happens that if two mirrors be placed so as to be exactly facing each other, the first will be reflected in the second and the second in the first. Now the first being reflected in the second carries to it is own image together with all the images which are represented in it, among these being the image of the second mirror; and so they continue from image to image on to infinity, in such a way that each mirror has an infinite number of mirrors within it, each smaller than the last, and one inside another.

By this example therefore, it is clearly proved that each thing transmits the image of itself to all those places where the thing itself is visible, and so conversely this object is able to receive into itself all the images of the things which are in front of it.